Sandbar Sunrise

A SUMMER COTTAGE NOVEL

REBECCA REGNIER

Text copyright ©2024
REBECCA REGNIER ALL RIGHTS RESERVED

No part of this book may be reproduced or transmitted in any form or by any means, electronic or mechanical, including photocopying, recording, or by any information storage and retrieval system, without the written permission of the author or publisher, except where permitted by law or for the use of brief quotations in a book review.
This is a work of fiction. Names, characters, businesses, places, events, and incidents are either the products of the author's imagination or used in a fictitious manner. Any resemblance to actual persons, living or dead, or actual events is purely coincidental.

Chapter One

J.J.

J.J. sat outdoors. She'd gotten a jump on the lunch crowd, but not a jump on the heat. It was already too warm for her taste. May in Haven Beach was apparently hotter than any day in August in her hometown.

But there was an ocean breeze and a view. This was J.J.'s first visit to the Gulf Coast of Florida. She liked the view. She loved the sound of the seashore. But she also felt intimidated.

The gentle waves turned into a roar sometimes. The salt stung J.J.'s skin. And well, sharks could just kiss right off.

Still, Seashell Shack had umbrellas and amazing views of the water. You really needed to kick off your shoes to eat there. Patrons were encouraged to leave a regular tip but also a seashell tip. The seashell tips stayed in the center of each table until the end of the day.

What bliss. The salt air, the hum of the surf, and the feeling that you were at the edge of the world made it magical here.

She wondered what Dean would think of this place.

Ugh. Dean. She'd traveled for the last nine months trying to get distance. J.J. thought a change of location would help her heal from the sudden loss of Dean, her husband of nearly thirty years. They'd missed that milestone by a few months.

Shoot.

J.J. shook her head to try to rearrange what was inside. It was easy for her to stay in a loop of the past. It was easy to replay her life with her husband and the kids. It was easy to get there, but it hurt the longer she stayed, and it was hard to get out.

She grabbed her shirt and pulled it down at the collar. It was too close to her throat. She tried to swallow. It was like her basic bodily functions stopped operating when she let herself think of Dean. Her loss took over and tried to choke her. J.J. reached out for the ice water the wait staff had brought to the table. She took a small sip.

The cool water opened her throat. She focused on the scene in front of her. A pelican swooped from a low point in the sky and plunged headfirst into the ocean.

Presumably, the bird had a fish in its beak. J.J. shifted her focus to a boat on the horizon. It was moving, but slowly. Her heartbeat slowed, too.

She got on top of her grief. That's what she'd really done the last nine months. Get on top of the wave that wanted to drown her.

J.J. had been up and down the East Coast. She'd flown out of Detroit at the end of the summer, only a few short weeks after burying Dean.

She visited New York City, Boston, and then moved down the coast as the weather turned from fall to winter.

Dean and J.J. weren't rich, but they did have life insurance. She always thought they had more than was necessary. Until it *was* necessary.

J.J.'s income from doing hair was their extra income. It was their vacation money. It was what they used when they needed something more. And it was what they saved for a rainy day.

It was Dean's construction business that paid the real bills. She knew her sons were trying to run it now, but how long that would last was anyone's guess.

The insurance payment she got was more money than she'd ever seen. For the first time in her life, she didn't have to worry about bouncing checks. You'd think that would be amazing. But she knew that wasn't going to last forever.

A little cash in the bank was cold comfort without Dean to laugh about it with. It turned out that being frugal wasn't something you got over. She may be on a "Grand Grief Tour," but she was still the J.J. who knew how to find a bargain and stretch a dollar.

On her grand tour, she'd visited Virginia, the Carolinas, Georgia, and as spring began, she made her way across Florida.

The name Haven Beach drew her.

Was she looking for a haven?

She'd been here for about a month, renting an efficient little apartment. She'd watched Spring Breakers come and go.

But it was probably time to move again. To where? She wasn't sure. J.J. didn't have a passport. Maybe that was next? Maybe she'd pretend she was Diane Lane and go under the Tuscan sun? But if the sun was the cure for what ailed her, it was taking its time working. Sun was in abundance here.

Her phone buzzed. J.J. had gotten into the habit of ignoring it. That was a positive development. But she was still a mom to the boys. And Jackie, her mom, was always one Pina Colada away from total chaos.

She'd visited Jackie here in Florida. She'd offered her mother the opportunity to stay in the house in Irish Hills as long as she wanted last year. But Jackie had a roaring social life at the Sunshine Vista Community. Jackie was happy at Sunshine Vista. She even had a snowbird boyfriend. God love Jackie Pawlak.

"The minute I see frost on the pumpkin, I'm out of here!" her mother said and was true to her word.

But the caller ID on her phone didn't list a familiar number. The display read *Barken Realty*.

J.J. picked up.

"Hello."

"J.J., It's Mary Barken!"

"Hi, Mary."

"We have a deal!"

J.J. had put the house she'd shared with Dean, their first house —her only house—on the market. They'd bought it from Jackie, actually, decades ago. That was how Jackie had afforded her snowbird lifestyle over the years. It wasn't extravagant, but social security, the house money, and her tiny place kept Jackie happy.

Dean had helped J.J. take care of Jackie. He never lost patience with Jackie and her weird demands.

"Already?" It had been up for sale for less than a month.

"Yep. I told you real estate was hot, hot, hot."

"Even after the tornado?"

"Oh, are you kidding me? That hasn't stopped Libby, Stone, or any big developers from sniffing around. And I got you ten grand above asking, thanks to the incredible upgrades Dean did."

"Stone Stirling?"

"Yeah, right? Strange bedfellows there. But yeah, he works with her all the time!"

Stone Stirling was Libby and J.J.'s arch nemesis. She wanted to ask a million questions, but this was about untangling from her old life, not sticking her nose back into Irish Hills.

"Well, what's next?" J.J. asked as she tried to process it. The house was sold. She wanted to move on, and here it was, another huge step forward.

"Well, you need to get your stuff packed, and I need to set a closing date with you. When can you be back?"

J.J. had not anticipated this part, the going back part. Was she ready to do that? The little grip she felt in the beat of her heart said no. She wasn't ready to go back.

"Could I do it from here, remotely?"

"Well, since you're going to be here to pack, I can schedule it all at once."

"It's just that...I'm unsure if I'll be back."

"Well, you can close from there, and I could hire a company to pack it up for you and put it in storage."

"How much does that cost?"

"Let me get an estimate, but I think you're going to spend the extra 10K I got you in the sale price to hire it out."

J.J. winced. Dean would lose it if he thought she was considering just hiring it out. They always did everything themselves. She could go back to enlist the boys. But the idea that it would just be taken care of, that she didn't have to sift through every memory and decide whether to throw it out or put it in storage felt easier. She wanted it easier.

"Let me get back to you on this. I need to think."

"Okay, but don't think too long. This family wants in before summer."

It was May, and summer was coming soon.

"Sure, sure, and great job on the sale."

J.J. put her phone on the table. She reached out and ran her finger along a shell that resembled the horn of a unicorn. It was bleached white.

She looked out at Haven Beach. An older couple, probably in their seventies, walked along the beach. They were holding hands. There was no hurry. The woman pointed to something on the sand, and the man picked it up for her. J.J.'s throat felt tight.

This was a beautiful place.

Back home, she'd be bombarded with memories. Here, she confronted a future that had slipped away, things she'd never get to do with Dean.

There was no right place.

"There you are."

A familiar voice distracted her from her melancholy.

She turned around. She knew this drill. She knew she was about to face some major pressure.

J.J. had been on the other side of it a few times.

Chapter Two

Libby

She'd waited long enough. Maybe D.J. had forgotten.

In the nine months since the tornado swept through Irish Hills, Libby had been busier than she'd ever been in her life. She'd found funds, made plans, cajoled the insurance company, and waited out a vicious winter that had halted construction projects.

She did all this without Dean Tucker. She missed Dean so much.

But D.J. Tucker had stepped up. He was taking a stab at running Tucker Construction in place of his dad. And it was working. Well, it was almost working.

Okay, it was working in the beginning, but not so much lately.

D.J. didn't have the vision yet, or the wealth of experience like Dean did. But there were moments when D.J. Tucker was more than the son of a great man. Libby saw it. She'd kept Tucker Construction as the main contractor for the downtown Irish Hills renovation project because of the man D.J. could almost be and because of his dad. She just didn't know how long her businesses could wait for D.J. Tucker to grow up.

D.J. was a big man, like Dean, but minus the beer gut. Though, from what Libby heard, D.J. was working on putting that gut on.

It wasn't her business. She was his boss and not his mom. Though she felt more like his aunt, thanks to how close she was to J.J.

Well, how close she used to be. J.J. had left them and was mostly ghosting everyone from Irish Hills.

Libby texted and tried to get J.J. on the phone all the time, but replies were random and sparse. J.J. Tucker had disappeared for all intents and purposes. And Libby was just so sad about that. Things were off balance without J.J. in their group and without J.J. in Libby's life.

J.J. could always see the humor. She was a cheerleader with an acerbic edge. She was the most grounded of them and yet the most likely to send them into peals of giggles.

But her friend needed to heal. Libby was trying to give her that, and at the same time, she held out hope that J.J. would find her way back.

J.J., the only one of them actually from Irish Hills, was the only one of them who didn't see Irish Hills as her happy ending.

That was an issue that dogged her, always under the surface. Could J.J. really be gone for good?

But more pressing, immediately pressing, was where in the heck was D.J. Tucker? They were supposed to meet in her office and talk about plans for interior walls for the buildings on the south side of Green Street.

The main drag of Irish Hills was getting very close to being ready for business on both sides of the street now.

Despite nature and the machinations of a billionaire, Irish Hills survived and thrived.

Hope's Table, Siena and Viv's Shop, the Mercantile, and now the new little bookshop had filled the spots.

Libby was using the last open spot on the south side of the main street as a temporary office, but would be happy to switch to the vacant spaces across the street. Work on the north side was underway. After last summer, there had been moments she'd feared they'd just have to level it.

But they fought to save this downtown, this whole community, and the fight was more potent than the tornado.

Which brought her back to D.J. Maybe he thought they were meeting on-site instead of her office?

Libby picked up her phone and decided to just walk over.

The tornado had gutted the buildings under construction on the Green Street intersection. It had put their work months, if not years, behind. But the worst damage was to Shelly's salon and the grocery store at both ends of the main drag.

Barton's Grocery was wiped out completely. Old Ned Barton died in his store, and Dean had died saving J.J. and Shelly.

Dean was now one of her main motivations to keep going. He'd done amazing things here. She wasn't going to quit until the whole state could see the legacy of his work.

Libby looked over at the grocery store.

It was one fine-looking building, and construction had been completed in record time.

Stone Stirling had hired the "best of the best," he'd said. He'd even hired a lot of local contractors. She wanted to hate his guts, but he kept doing honorable things. Still...

Libby was wary when Stirling bought the place. She'd actually tried to punch the man. But since then, there'd been a truce. A grudging one.

Stone had been good for Irish Hills after the tornado hit. That didn't mean she trusted the man—it just meant that his grocery store was good and needed; and had helped keep tourists booking cottages and homes for this summer's season. Yet Libby feared there was another shoe to drop when it came to Stone's encroachment.

Libby made her way across the street. The buildings, connected in some cases and separated by two little alleys at each end, were in various stages of development and construction.

In her mind's eye, she could see the destruction of last summer. Even with all the work they'd tried to do since.

The tornado and winds had ripped off much of the roofs that Dean had installed. The vintage exterior brick, so painstakingly selected by Dean, had crumbled down in a heap on the front side of the stretch of buildings. The display windows had shattered as if a bomb had exploded inside the structures.

Every nail that Dean had pounded in had twisted out. Several downspouts he'd installed were found on the lakeshore at the end of downtown. They were mangled and twisted like pretzels. The rotation of the wind bent metal, tree limbs, and whatever else it scooped up and flung all over the county.

A tornado doesn't go in a straight line. It darts and turns. Last summer's twister danced like a dervish, leaving one side of the street intact and decimating the other just feet away.

D.J. Tucker supervised the initial cleanup. Libby saw him try to manage his shock and grief by diving headfirst into running his dad's business.

They moved from cleanup to roofing, fixing brick, and replacing walls. It was a chaotic tumble forward, but they had gotten it done. And now the project focused on the interior of each space.

There was still so much to do before Libby could market the redeveloped block to tenants to sign leases. If she thought too much about it, she'd need a nap. Libby functioned best when she was busy and when chaos nipped at her heels, as it had done since the twister hit.

Libby arrived at the block's far end to find the anchor building's service door unlocked. That probably did mean that D.J. was already here. She stepped inside. Electrical wiring was on the to-do list. Luckily, the sun was already bright this morning.

"D.J.," she called out, but no answer.

This stretch was similar to the one across the street in that there were several spaces to lease that could house any number of businesses. They had five across the street. Here, they had two more; seven potential spaces to fill.

If Libby could rent or even sell these to vibrant tenants, it would be mission accomplished. She had stretched the insurance payout as far as she could to make it happen. Money was running out. She needed to finish this and get income here this summer.

D.J.'s tool belt was on the floor in the center of the space. That was odd. Libby went up the stairs to the second-floor loft, where the mystery of the missing D.J. was solved.

An empty bottle of whiskey sat next to a very full D.J. Tucker. Libby's heart lurched for a second, seeing him there. But then a snore that sounded more like a truck passing by than human respiration let her know that D.J. was breathing. He was sleeping that whiskey off on their job site.

He wasn't dead. That was something.

D.J. Tucker was a man on the edge of an amazing life or total disaster. Right now, disaster was winning.

Libby kneeled next to the wayward contractor and nudged him on the shoulder.

"D.J., wake up."

He made an indecipherable sound and rolled over. She heard a buzzing noise on the other side of the massive amount of man that was D.J. Tucker.

It was his phone, likely buzzing with messages from her. It was rattling the subfloor. She went over and picked it up.

And there, on the screen, was a picture of J.J.

Aha. She's called her son.

Out of curiosity, Libby clicked on the photo. And there it was. The current location of J.J. Tucker.

Libby decided it was time to bring J.J. back. If not for Irish Hills, for her son.

And now, she knew right where to go to make it happen.

* * *

Less than twenty-four hours later, Libby was on Haven Beach. It was odd. Slightly beat up, but with a vintage vibe that was so different from most of the Gulf Coast. She'd never heard of it before. It had to be one of the few remaining "old Florida" communities left in the state. It really felt like a beach town. Not so different from Irish Hills—if Irish Hills didn't have the biting winter and slightly less biting spring.

Leave it to J.J. to find it, of course.

There was a distractingly handsome man running the tiny reception office.

"I'm looking for the woman renting that end unit, J.J. Tucker?"

"Ah, she's hilarious, tiny but potent, eh?"

Libby got protective. *Was this man interested in J.J.?*

"Yes, that's her."

"Smallest peppers pack the most spice, you know?'"

"Yeah, I hear, so J.J.?"

"She loves The Seashell Shack. I'd check there first."

"Will do, thanks."

Libby left the Laird Hamilton-looking surfer receptionist to go find J.J.

The Seashell Shack was a few buildings over, but right on the beach. It was easy to see why J.J. liked it.

Libby needed to push Keith to open the restaurant at Steve's Marina. Eating on the water is so cool! He was close, but as with everything, Libby wanted it done yesterday to lure and keep the summer visitors.

Libby saw J.J. before J.J. knew she was there. J.J.'s choppy haircut had grown out a bit. She was tan. She sat alone, nursing a cold drink.

Libby's heart leaped in her chest to see J.J., and now it was time to do whatever she could to get J.J. to come home.

She walked up behind her.

"There you are."

J.J. turned and, recognizing Libby, answered back with her signature sass. "Whatever it is, no. My answer is no."

"What if the question is, does this place have good crab cakes?"

"Well, in that case, yes, but anything else you're going to throw at me, it's a no."

"Then I won't ask to sit down. I'll just do it."

Libby threw her leg over the picnic table bench seat, the umbrella offering welcome shade from the sun's heat.

"I'm not kidding, Libby; I know your moves."

"Look, at the very least, let me sit under this umbrella. Redheads are not designed for Florida. Sun in May? I'm probably already blistering."

"Ugh. You look good. Too good. You realize this is a t-shirt and flip-flop joint?"

"Thanks, and yeah, the wedges and tailored pants are overkill, no question."

Seated across from her friend, Libby had a million things to tell and ask her, and she was ready to make her case. But seeing J.J.—different, but the same, familiar but somehow alien in this space and out of context—gave her pause.

They stopped trading barbs for a beat. Libby put her hand across the table and covered J.J.'s. She squeezed gently. They didn't need to go on and on. She didn't need to offer condolences or find words to tell her friend that she missed her or that she wanted to help. J.J. knew that.

Libby knew J.J. would feel the same if the roles were reversed. In fact, they *had been* reversed when they first reconnected. J.J. had helped Libby figure out her second act. J.J. was the touchstone Libby needed.

But Libby knew that if she said any of those things in her heart right now, she'd start to cry, and they didn't have time for that.

Chapter Three

J.J.

J.J. had been on the other side of this pitch. Libby was the queen of getting people to come to Irish Hills. And J.J. had been her enthusiastic sidekick.

J.J. put a hand up to try to stop the spiel before it got started.

"I know you want a salon. I'm the only one to do it. You need it fast, but you will help me."

Libby's eyes went wide, as if she'd never even considered the idea. "Well, do you want to open a salon?"

"No."

"I will say, we're all driving into Ann Arbor to get the works. Not ideal. You would be the best person to fill that niche in Irish Hills. Shelly is retired, so no worries there."

J.J. inspected Libby's hair. After thirty years of doing hair, old habits died hard. "Your hair is a little, well..." J.J. pointed to Libby's gray roots. She was due. That was clear.

"I came here to talk to you instead of driving straight to the salon. That's how serious things are."

"Libby, I know your moves. Let's remember, I'm not an expert in my field or an award-winning anything, okay?"

"I do not want to hear you downplay yourself."

"It isn't that, it's just—" She stopped.

"You know, all of us Sandbar Sisters were from somewhere and then went out in the world. You didn't. You have every right to explore, well, anything you want. Especially after what you went through. We all understand. We miss you. We want to be there for you, but we get it. Being away was what you needed."

"Thank you. Yeah, I did a lot of exploring. I had to learn that I could. It was always me and Dean and the boys, and then me and Dean. I don't think I ever rented a hotel room on my own until last year. Can you imagine?"

"So, how are you doing?"

J.J. paused.

The waitress approached, and Libby ordered. "I'll have the Cuban also if that's okay."

"They're spectacular. Best choice."

The waitress left. And J.J. still didn't have a good answer to Libby's question.

"I'm okay. It comes in waves, but I hear that's how this goes. I've seen everything from Times Square to a school of dolphins, so that's something."

"It is something!"

"Okay, so you can go back to Irish Hills and let them all know I'm alive and quasi-well."

"Actually, you're really going to have to come back with me," Libby said. And she had a look.

J.J. had seen it many times. There was a determination in Libby Quinn that was scary if you were in her way and inspiring if you were on her side. J.J. wondered which one it was. She was not ready to save the town again. Maybe she was in Libby's way right now. J.J. felt goosebumps rise on her arms. This was what it was like to know Libby had you in her sight and was about to pull the trigger.

"You've got plenty of powerhouse women to save Irish Hills," J.J. pointed out. "I know this better than anyone."

"We need you, yes, and I'd like nothing more than to talk business and world domination, but it's your family that needs attention."

J.J.'s heart rate spiked immediately.

"What? Is everyone okay? I got a text from Austin last night, and D.J., uh..." J.J. opened her phone. *When did I last heard from D.J.?* She scrolled through her messages in a panic.

Libby put her hand on J.J.'s.

"Calm down, they're okay, but it is D.J. I'm really worried about him."

"What?"

Libby was reluctant all of a sudden. The hard-charging dealmaker receded, and J.J. watched Libby squirm a little in her seat. The waitress showed up again; this time, it was Libby who looked grateful for the momentary interruption.

The food in front of her, waitress gone, J.J. couldn't wait any longer. "Spill it."

"I think—no, I *know*—that D.J. has a terrible drinking problem. And I think you need to try to get him into AA or something."

J.J. took a breath and let it out with a sigh. And then she remembered. "Darn, looks like he takes after his dad more than I realized."

Libby cocked her head.

There were decades when J.J. and Libby had not been in each other's lives, a part of J.J. and Dean's story that Libby had no knowledge of.

After hearing about D.J., it was that part that came flooding right back to J.J.

. . .

1998 - J.J.

J.J. was only four months along.

So why, oh why, does it look like I'm in my third trimester already?

She lay on her side and tried to grab sleep. But an intense focus on sleep is not how to get there. She was lying in bed and about as far away from relaxed as you could be.

D.J. was three years old and usually slept through the night. But Dean had promised to take him to see *Mulan* and instead took him to see *Armageddon*. The poor kid was worried a giant Gastroid, as he called it, was going to land on Playdoodle Preschool.

She'd spent the first part of the night assuring him that they weren't going to be hit by a Gastroid and the second part trying not to feel whoever was in her belly kicking her.

Ugh. Dean. He made it seem like he was going to take care of everything, but lately, nothing was getting done. Just today, she had to make a special trip to get cash to pay for Playdoodle.

After she'd asked him three times, Dean had forgotten to do it.

She tried not to take evening appointments, but Shelly pushed her to open her book for the evenings: "It's two weeks before Christmas. Everyone needs their roots done. I know you can use the extra."

Shelly was right, they could use the extra. J.J.'s days were stretched to the max already, but the evening clients were the extra money she needed.

There was so much that they needed to do for the house. It was new to them, but it was still Jackie's old disaster. It needed so much work, which was why they could afford it.

Even if Dean did the work himself, the roof would easily cost a couple of thousand bucks.

So, she did two colors and one cut this evening. She was exhausted. But also wide awake.

J.J. turned over to her other side with considerable effort. She was excited for D.J. to have a little brother or sister. But she was not a good pregnant woman. Everything felt alien. At least the first time around, she'd had months and months before she even looked preggers. This time, well, the basketball was turning into a beach ball with every passing day. This baby was Tucker-sized from the get-go.

But luckily, D.J. was finally sleeping. J.J. slowly drifted into rest, even if it wasn't deep sleep.

Dean was out with his buddies. If he woke up D.J. when he stumbled in, well, he could deal with it.

When the phone rang, J.J. looked at her bedside alarm clock.

It was three in the morning. *Did I sleep, even two hours?* That was something, at least.

The phone rang again.

She picked it up and struggled to use her elbows to get into an upright position.

"Hello?"

"Hey, J.J., it's Earl Shot."

Earl was a Lenawee County Sheriff's Deputy who worked in Irish Hills. J.J. went from half asleep to fully awake and ready to throw up.

"I'm sorry to wake ya. I know you're preggers again, but, uh. I have Dean here."

"What, oh my God, is he dead?"

"No, sorry, didn't mean to scare you that way. He's alive. He's okay."

"Good, okay, wow."

"But it's not all good."

Earl was an old friend. He was a family friend. He'd even dated Jackie once or twice. He'd showed up to this very house to help scare off a few of her more aggressive admirers. Jackie should have married Earl Shot, J.J. often thought. But he was too stable to be attractive to her chaotic mom.

"It's okay, Earl. What's happened?"

"Uh, Dean got a bit, over-served over at the Wagon Wheel. And then he got, uh, belligerent about whether or not soccer was a real sport."

"Oh, Lord."

"He doesn't think it is, if you're wondering."

"I've heard, yeah, okay. Is he under arrest?"

"Yeah, there was a brawl. He threw a punch, not just him, I'm told. But by the time I got there, it was confusing."

"I bet, but I can get him?"

"Yeah, they'll ask you to post. He's going to be charged with assault, probably."

"Thanks for the heads up, I'm on my way."

"Well, drive safe. He's asleep last I checked."

J.J. debated what to do. A big part of her wanted to leave Dean there and get him later after she'd dropped D.J. at Playdoodle. But she didn't. She got up. She found her maternity leggings, her stupid pink maternity t-shirt, and a sweater that didn't button over her stomach. She packed a few things for D.J. and then went to his room.

"Mama, what's happening? Is it the gastroid?"

"No, honey, no, we have to go get Daddy. He needs a ride home."

"Okay."

She hoisted D.J. up. At three, he was already forty-five pounds. His legs dangled, and his feet nearly came to her knees as he snuggled his head on her shoulder. This boy was going to be bigger than her before he hit middle school, no doubt.

They walked out into the night air. J.J. maneuvered D.J. into the car seat, and he fell back into a deep sleep. That was something. She was envious. She couldn't imagine falling back asleep now, even in her bed.

D.J. was an angel through it all. He sat in the chair in the waiting room. He walked with her to where they'd release Dean, and instead of asking her to pick him up again as they waited, he wanted to slide down to the floor and catch a few more z's.

She thought the floor looked gross. So, her pregnant self picked up her gigantic son and rocked side to side as they waited for his gigantic drunken dad to be released.

A big garage-style rolling door opened. J.J. watched as the assortment of men who'd been arrested overnight stood, waiting to get out, waiting to be processed. It wasn't that different than a pen of steer milling around at the Lenawee County Fair.

Dean walked toward her.

She didn't say anything. This wasn't the first screw-up. Or the second. Dean Tucker was the best boyfriend, a loving dad, and a talented, hard-working man, but he was an alcoholic. She knew that, but he didn't.

J.J. had made a choice when she posted bail. It was a decision solidified as she drove to get her husband.

This was it. This was the last straw. No ultimatum. No big fight. She was going to drop him at home. Drop D.J. at school and then get her stuff. They'd move into her brother's apartment for a bit until she could find a place.

D.J. woke up and lifted his head from her shoulder. "Daddy!"

Dean made a gesture to take their son and carry him to the car. J.J. turned her shoulder so he could not. *Let him see what I'm carrying*, she thought.

They got in the car.

"I'm assuming your truck is over at the Wagon Wheel parking lot?"

"Yes."

She headed to the bar. She hoped it hadn't been towed. That would be another expense.

They were both quiet. D.J. peppered her with a few questions about getting McDonald's for breakfast. She agreed.

"After we drop Daddy off." She wasn't interested in eating with Dean. Or chatting. Or hearing his side of things.

They pulled into the parking lot of the Wagon Wheel.

"I'm assuming you're okay to drive?"

"Yeah, worn off now."

"Great."

Dean grabbed the handle of the car door. He cracked it open. And then stopped. "I'm never gonna drink again, I promise you."

J.J. looked at him for the first time. *Really* looked at him.

His hair was a mess, disheveled, and he needed it cut. His beard probably smelled like beer. She didn't plan to get closer to find out. But when she looked into his eyes, they were bloodshot. They weren't, however, unfocused.

There was determination in his gaze. And there was honesty, an honesty that had been missing when it came to his drinking. An honesty he'd shrunk from or batted down when she'd tried to show him the truth.

Dean had never made this promise before. He'd never even acknowledged that their problems mostly occurred after he'd had one or a dozen too many.

The honest man, the hard worker that was his daytime self, *that* was who she'd married.

She loved the way he looked. His strength. His humor.

She loved the parts of him that he'd passed down to D.J.

J.J. changed her plans. She kept her hands on the wheel but locked eyes with her husband. And then she made a promise of her own:

"I'm not in the business of chances or ultimatums. Not when it's this serious. I'm not going to nag you or chase after a life I am supposed to have, or my kids are supposed to have. I'm getting the life we deserve, with or without you. You keep that promise, or I promise you, D.J. and I are out of here that day. That first whiff. As fast as this Escort Wagon can drive me."

"I love you, J.J., and our family. So much."

"Yeah? Words. We'll see if you can back it up. And that's it. I'm not going to yell at you or parent you. I love you, too. But I'm mama to that one, not you. Got it? And that's it. We're done talking about it. And I promise you this, too, here's the second gift. I'm not holding this against you. It's done."

That was the other thing that would break them, a grudge. If she held this over his head forever, he may as well keep drinking because they'd not have any peace.

Dean took the medicine she doled.

He got out of the car and walked to his truck.

They drove to McDonald's, mother and son. D.J. enjoyed his drive-through breakfast. And J.J. worked on fixing her attitude, on letting go of the anger she'd held tight to since she'd found out she was pregnant again.

J.J. knew it was going to be hard not to harangue Dean. But any chance they had of a happy marriage depended on both of them living up to their promises that morning in the Wagon Wheel Saloon parking lot.

Present Day

J.J. told some of the story to Libby. Libby listened.

"I know you had bumpy patches in the beginning. You said as much. Did he keep the promise?"

J.J. thought about it.

"We were married nearly thirty years. And that was the beginning. We'd have a million scenarios and promises and knock down drag-outs between then and now."

"Gotcha."

J.J. didn't elaborate. There were moments when J.J. didn't think her marriage would last. And others where it was J.J.'s attitude and actions that deserved a come to Jesus moment.

It was a life, it was decades of partnership, it was messy. But it was all gone now.

Ugh. Dean.

"Well, you did it," J.J. conceded. "I didn't think you could do it. But you did it. Sending D.J. a howler won't cut it."

"I thought you weren't in the business of healing someone else's addiction?"

"I said I wasn't there to police my husband. But my son? You can bet your Ann Taylor sweater set that I'm going to harangue him."

"So, you're coming back to Irish Hills?" Libby enthused.

"For now. I've got a son to kick in the butt and a house to close on."

"Oh, we'll find you a new one, don't you worry."

"Stop, this is temporary. This is a fire I'm putting out. I'm not joining your cult of lady business-owner do-gooders. I'm still—I hate to say this—I'm in mourning. It sounds so old or something, but I'm not ready to move on. I am still firmly married to Dean Tucker even though he's rudely decided to take his leave early." J.J. blinked away tears. Dean should be the one kicking their son's backside. That would be helpful right now.

"Think of it as moving forward," Libby said gently, "not moving on, and it doesn't mean forgetting Dean."

"You're selling me. Stop selling me. I'm immune."

Libby smiled. J.J. knew it was a victory smile.

Chapter Four

J.J.

J.J. shouldn't be scared. *Why in the world am I scared?* But she was. Libby drove her home, and as they approached town, she felt her stomach tighten.

This was her hometown. She'd lived her entire life short of the last nine months. Libby turned onto Green Street.

J.J. shuddered. This was ridiculous. *Get it together, Tucker.*

"Are you okay?"

"I'm weirdly freaked."

As they drove into town, things felt familiar. Normal. As comfortable as her favorite slippers. The shops along the north side of Green looked beautiful. She knew it was all Libby, but maybe she had a little part in making this happen. Hope's restaurant was bustling, even so early in the season.

"I'm so proud of Hope. Aren't you so proud of Hope?" As she said this, J.J.'s fear receded. She was so happy for her friend. Of all of them, Hope had one of the rougher times with her ex before moving back to Irish Hills. Hope's dreams were the longest delayed, but now they blossomed.

"Honey, heck yes, she's a goddess at that place."

"We'll get dinner while I'm in town."

"If we can get a table."

"Right?" J.J. said and again, felt pride, that Hope was living this dream, and J.J. had been an accomplice to it.

She had given Libby crap about having ulterior motives and trying to lure J.J. into a business venture. Still, J.J. had been with Libby the whole way. And seeing Hope's, and then the boutique, and mercantile, it almost felt like they were her babies too!

"Okay, yeah, the south side of Green, though, we're behind."

J.J. looked across the street, avoiding the center of it. She didn't want to see the gazebo. She also avoided looking to the end of the street, her old salon. *The place that—no!* She put a hard stop to her last memory of the salon.

J.J. turned her attention to the future. She knew one question was all it took to get Libby to go on and on about plans for Irish Hills.

"Oh, okay, yeah, so where are you on that?"

J.J. had planned to show no interest. She knew Libby, given an inch, would take a mile. That was great when the two were in step, but J.J. was out of step. Now J.J.'s plan went out the window. She needed distraction from the memories that drove her out of this town.

As they took a loop around the main street to get a better view of the south side of Green, the question answered itself.

The roof was done. That was good.

"D.J. took on the roof project right away, a very strong start. And I was struggling to get the insurance funds. I used credit cards to pay for some of the materials we needed. It was a tough slog in the fall. But we got it done before the winter. That was key."

"Good on D.J. for that. But we've got boarded windows. Where's the sidewalk?"

"Yeah, that's just the stuff you can see on the outside. Inside, we're working on electric and plumbing, and it's, ugh...I hate to say this about D.J."

"It's okay, spill it."

"He's great half the time, and his work is impeccable when he completes it." J.J. could feel Libby's discomfort with the next part, but J.J. had asked for it. "He's unreliable, and he's also bad at managing his subs."

Libby was direct even though she was gripping the steering wheel and furrowing her brow as she told the truth, as she saw it, about D.J.

J.J. didn't like hearing bad stuff about her kids. No mother did. But she also wasn't a woman who wanted sugar-coating. She didn't give it and didn't want to get it. J.J. put her hand on Libby's shoulder to try to ease the tension of the moment.

"Look, it's okay," J.J. reassured her, "that's why I'm here."

"I'm so glad you are. I think that's going to change the game. I do."

Libby had shared that she'd found D.J. passed out on the job the other day. It made J.J. wince, but it was the unvarnished truth.

"The good news is that the insurance money is finally in," Libby continued, "and I can mostly pay for the repairs. If we could get on track with them, this could be ready to go this summer. Late summer, but still. I do need to get revenue in here."

"I do know that drill." J.J. had helped ensure that the vacancies didn't stay vacant for long over the last few seasons.

"Great, okay, yes." Libby patted the steering wheel. Being on the back foot wasn't her standard position.

Just then, the new building at the end of the street caught J.J.'s eye.

"That's nuts! The grocery store looks amazing."

"Yeah, that's been one of the biggest things that has changed around here."

"Is it open?"

"Actually, grand opening this weekend, soft-open now."

"Did the Barons put this together? I always thought only Ned was interested in the store."

"Yeah, he was, rest his soul, and his family wasn't. They cashed out to, uh, believe it or not, Stone Stirling."

"What?"

"Yeah, I nearly punched him in the face when I heard."

"I would have done the same."

"Yeah, he brought and did some dealing with the Freshy Market people. It's one of the most gorgeous grocery stores you've ever seen."

"But it's Stone Stirling. He's worming his way in! We won, he can't do this! How in the world...?"

"Look, the guy isn't all bad."

J.J. raised her eyebrows. "Who am I talking to? What have you done with the real Libby?"

"No, no, it's taken time, but he's done everything we asked for in terms of this location. He hasn't overstepped or asked to take over the town or tear it down. This time, it looks like he just wants to help."

"Yeah, I'm not buying it."

J.J. wanted to shake Libby. *How can she, or anyone, trust Stone Stirling after he tried to wipe Irish Hills off the map?*

"Even Aunt Emma seems to like him, and she's a tough sell."

J.J. shook her head. This wasn't her problem. This wasn't her circus or her monkeys anymore. Well, D.J. was her monkey; her sloppy, hard-drinking monkey. She'd focus on that.

* * *

They finished the mini tour of Irish Hills and they pulled into J.J.'s neighborhood a block off of Green Street. She grew up here. It was the Townie section of Irish Hills. The big money and the vacation crowd didn't hang out here back then. It was up to J.J. to find kids to play with, and she did. She'd found her Sandbar Sisters.

The neighborhood was going through a change. Again, she thought of Dean. He'd turned their old ranch house into a great place to live. Their work had upped the property values on the block, and now it is a charming street with one tidy ranch after another. This was a cute place for young families or even retired couples. Ranch homes went out of style, but Dean always said they were the perfect floor plan.

"You watch," he'd say, "you get over fifty, you want a main floor, everything. You have little rugrats, you want bedrooms close by and a big basement. The ranch is an underappreciated situation, mark my words."

He was right.

This was it. This was why she was sick to her stomach with worry. She'd run away from this house in the wake of Dean's death. And now they were pulling into the driveway. She was going to have to deal with it. The real estate sign in the yard proclaimed the house sale was pending.

There was a lockbox on the door.

"Do you want to do this on your own?"

"Actually, no. Do you mind?"

"You don't even need to ask."

J.J. would borrow Libby's strength for the next bit.

She would stay a few days, get the place cleaned out, get her son straightened out, and then, she'd...

She didn't know what. But it would come to her.

The house had been mostly decluttered, cleaned out, and staged for sale. But walking in, a flood of emotion threatened to pull J.J. underwater.

"It looks great in here," Libby said.

"Yep." J.J. didn't have words.

Libby stepped back, and J.J. took several more steps forward.

Dean at the table with the boys, that scene, repeated over and over, flashed into her brain:

"We need meat and potatoes and a vegetable."

That was the order from Dean when J.J. would just as happily give everyone a bowl of Apple Jacks for dinner. She was glad now that they'd done that, that they'd had family dinners.

She had a trove of dinners to unpack in her memories. But not yet. She couldn't look at those times with Dean. When her boys were little, and her husband was here.

"I think I'm not ready," J.J. said. Her own voice sounded shaky to her. She didn't want to be shaky.

"You don't have to be. Let's just do a quick walkabout, and I'll find a company to move the stuff. You don't have to do a thing." Libby wanted to solve problems. That was her art, her mission.

J.J. didn't want to be this dependent person, this basket case. She was never the basket case; she held the basket and scooped the messes other people made into it. That's who she was.

But now, in her fifties, she didn't know who she was anymore.

She did know that she had to face this. She had to pull herself together.

"No, no. Dean would absolutely call me a baby if he saw this display. I need to get on with it."

"You're used to doing everything yourself; you don't have to, and you're not being a baby. And if you don't remember, Dean wanted, above all things, to make sure you were happy."

J.J. took a breath. "Okay, well, let's walk through. We can do that, and I can see what's what."

A tour of the three-bedroom ranch home didn't take long. There was no east wing or west wing. There was a front room, a kitchen, and a family room behind that. There were three bedrooms, one full bath, and a powder room. The full basement was the salvation of J.J.'s sanity. Toys and a bathroom with a shower for the boys helped J.J. survive being outnumbered.

She made all of them shower down there. They did as she

asked. She knew now that, really, they'd treated her like a queen. She didn't know it then; she only realized now that their cozy little kingdom was gone.

She heard her boys laughing, Dean humming Johnny Cash as he went to work in the morning. That's how these walls talked to her.

They were crowded in here as a family, but once the boys grew up, this was just the right amount of space for Dean and J.J. as empty nesters.

"You know, I never would have moved. I was about to turn Austin's room into a workout space, and D.J.'s was going to get a makeover for my mom to use when she was in town."

"It's a lovely house. It shows Dean's craftmanship in every square inch."

"It wasn't always so lovely. But it had a good foundation, Dean always said."

After walking from room to room and assessing the garage and basement, J.J. calmed down a bit. She didn't want to pack up her past, but she would do it. She'd feared being here, but she'd managed to do it.

"So, do you want me to call around to get a moving company on this? Where are we going to have them store things? There's a place in Adrian."

"Actually, Libby, I'm going to do it. I have to do it."

"Are you sure?"

"I am. It might even help."

"Whatever you need."

"What I need...Well, I can pack up what's left in this house. I think it will take about a week. What I'm sure of is that I don't want to stay in this house. An empty nest is one thing, but a lonely widow is something else. I don't want to be here as that."

"Oh, please stay with me at Nora House. You know I have more room than I need, more room than a dozen people need."

"Are you sure?"

"Of course, make Nora House your new home base. I'd love that!!"

"Now you're looking like you've won something. This makes me nervous."

"No, no, just we're going to have a little party, just for all of us to get together, and then maybe a sun day if the May weather cooperates, and—"

"Cool your jets. I said I'd stay for a week. Stop whatever is going on in there." J.J. pointed to Libby's forehead.

"Oh, no big plans, nothing at all."

"Right."

J.J. was going to pack this house up herself, but she wasn't going to sleep in the bed or rifle through the kitchen remembering meals gone by. *Nope, not doing it.*

"I still have a car in the garage. If D.J. started it once in a while I should be okay to drive to your place."

"Let's check."

The car started, the plan was in place, and Libby was happy as a clam at what she thought was her victory.

"I'm going to do some work here, see if I can catch up with D.J., and then swing by the new grocery store, much as I hate the idea."

"I mean, it's pretty awesome. Stone notwithstanding. Anyway, I've got to get to the office too. Just head to Nora House whenever. Keith's coming over later. He's going to check on my little outboard. It wasn't starting the other day."

"Is that a metaphor?"

"J.J., no!"

"Sure, sure, look, don't worry about me. Have him check your outboard or tonsils or whatever you two geriatric love birds have planned. I'm going to be a while."

It was fun to see how easily Libby could still blush, redhead at the core.

"I'll put you in the old game room, side door open."

"And Libby? You don't have to babysit me. I'm cool."

"Okay, okay. Let me know if you need anything. Anything."

"Who's the townie here, anyway?"

"I know, you're right."

They hugged goodbye, and J.J. was actually happy to be alone for a bit. After all these months of nomadic life, she'd gotten somewhat used to that.

"Well, Dean, you win. You made it so I'm the one who has to clean up all our stuff." She said it out loud to no one. Unless he was hovering around like the movie *Ghost*. It made her laugh to think that. Dean as Patrick Swayze.

Dean had been the neat one, and J.J. the pack rat. If she had gone first, he'd have had a lot of annoying chores to do. As it stood, they'd done a lot to purge over the years, but now it was the last of it. The last of them.

But before she turned a cold eye to the remains of their accumulated stuff, she had a son to wrangle.

It would be a week of trying not to be haunted by the past. The very out-of-whack present would be just the counterbalance she needed.

Chapter Five

J.J. had to check in with her brother, wayward sons, and real estate agent. She also wanted to connect with the rest of the Sandbar Sisters. But after the travel, a walkthrough of the house, and realizing that there was still a decent amount of work to do to get it empty, she was feeling tired. The task she had ahead might be overwhelming.

Her confidence in Libby might have been premature.

Part of her worried that she shouldn't have sold the house. If she let the place sit here, she wouldn't be forced to do a thing with it.

Except she wasn't a dummy, and Dean would have scolded her, too, on this. The market was hot in Irish Hills. She could get three times what they paid for it if she sold it now. She'd seen a lot of ups and downs in Michigan, enough to know to strike while the iron was hot.

The insurance from Dean and the cash from the house would provide some money to give her time to decide what she wanted to do when she grew up.

She locked up the house and pocketed a list of things she needed both for cleanup and to take over to Nora House.

J.J. decided a trip to the new grocery store would be the way to wrap up her day. It was all she could manage. The trip from Florida was one thing. The trip down memory lane was the real reason she felt exhausted.

J.J. knew she had to deal with D.J., but, in the words of Scarlett O'Hara, she'd think about that tomorrow.

Again, her old station wagon started on the first try. What do you know about that? *Dean, all the way, again.* He'd gotten the oil changes, the fluid checks, and the millions of little maintenance details that kept the thing running.

She drove over to Barton's Food Village, or what used to be Barton's, and was amazed at the number of cars in the parking lot.

The sleepy village of Irish Hills was wide awake, even in May, which was traditionally too early for the "season."

After she parked, she looked up at the new Irish Hills Village Market sign.

Sometimes, J.J. felt like the only one who'd lost something during the tornado. It was selfish. She knew it was. The truth was that Ned Barton, Shelly's salon, and all the work that had gone into downtown had been blown away; everyone was touched when tragedy hit a small town. Seeing the new building, so different from what was here before, reminded J.J. that the winds blew apart more lives than just hers. It helped her stop feeling so sorry for herself.

In the wake of Dean's death, she'd had to get away and process things her way. Being back, though, she wondered if she'd delayed actually processing her grief. *Was it wrong to have left?* Other people did it all the time. But maybe she had only avoided the pain or dodged a bullet. Well, she *thought* she had done that. Dodged it. But she had not. This grief wasn't a bullet to be dodged. It was a heat-seeking missile.

J.J. looked up at the gorgeous new grocery store that had replaced the old, rickety Barton's Food Village.

Ned was dead, the old store gone. This wasn't just her loss. She had shopped in this spot hundreds, thousands of times. As a young mom, she'd pushed a cart with Austin in a baby carrier and D.J. in the basket. Ned Barton wasn't one to buy the fancy racecar-shaped grocery carts.

She remembered D.J. sweetly sitting there as she handed him groceries. He'd arrange the stuff around his perch in the corner of the cart.

Back in those days, they were trying to spend sixty dollars a week on groceries. She remembered debates, to put it mildly, with Dean about how she chose to stretch those sixty bucks.

"What is this? Windex? Toilet bowl cleaner? This is supposed to be a grocery trip."

"Uh, yeah, those *are* groceries."

She'd unload the bags, and Dean would pace around, wounded, as he observed her grocery selections.

"These are cleaning products. You can't *eat* cleaning products for dinner."

"Well, keep that attitude up, and you'll get a thermos of glass cleaner in your lunch box." She smiled and ignored Dean's critique. "And you can go next week and take the kids."

She'd thought Dean would balk at that, but he hadn't. He'd gone the next week and learned all about the challenges of a shoestring budget and shopping with two babies.

"By the time I got the diapers and formula, I'd used seventy-five percent of our budget."

"You don't say?"

"You win. You're way better than I am at this."

And that was the last time she heard a complaint about her grocery haul. Well, sometimes she caught heck for generic peanut butter, but she could take it.

Those days seemed so hectic, sometimes even a blur. Now, though, before she walked into the fancy new grocery store, she knew she missed those shoestring budget days. She could almost see her two sweet but gigantic sons holding her groceries as the three of them navigated through the aisles.

She closed her eyes a beat.

J.J. was trying hard to get to a place where she could smile at her memories. She wasn't there yet. She felt pain when that grocery shopping memory popped up. If Dean was here, if he saw this fancy new place, they would reminisce about the old days of sky-high baby formula, diapers, Hamburger Helper, and cleaning products.

"Ugh, you're here to get some wine and cheese and garbage bags. Snap out of it," J.J. mumbled to herself. She forged ahead into the new store.

"Toto, we're not in Barton's anymore," she said out loud, of course, and took in the gloriousness of Irish Hills Village Market. There were high beamed ceilings, rows and rows of packaged foods, colorful towers of fresh produce, a deli, and a bakery. The building went on as far as the eye could see. J.J. had to remind herself she was in Irish Hills. This place looked a lot like the fancy grocery store she'd accidentally walked into in Connecticut while searching for a pack of Twizzlers.

J.J. got to work filling her cart, first with supplies for boxing up the house—garbage bags, and, of course, Windex to wipe down the last things that needed wiping down after she emptied cabinets. She'd have to stop in and see her brother and get some Goo Gone, too. There were sticky things yet to be dislodged, she was sure.

Then she wondered about boxes. She knew most stores had loads of boxes they didn't need, though by the looks of this place, the boxes were probably lined in cashmere.

J.J. finished the house aisle and perused the produce. *Man, this is too much!* She decided on a brick of cheese, a bottle of wine, some crackers, and a lovely bunch of grapes. She may have grown up on the wrong side of the tracks, but she knew enough not to come empty-handed to Nora House.

Shopping complete, she played her hunch and found the produce manager.

"Do you have any extra boxes in the back I could have for moving?"

"Sure do!" The produce manager was young, energetic, and cheerful as he bounded away while she waited.

Moments later, the friendly kid returned with six lovely boxes for her upcoming project. *Ha, free of charge. Take that, Dean Tucker!*

Ugh, Dean isn't here.

She thanked the manager for the boxes, checked out, and refused a lovely offer to help her to her car. She was probably too defensive; it seemed like a thing an elderly widow would need, help out to the car.

"No, no, thank you. I can manage."

Ned Barton would choke if he realized there was a full-time bagger at this store and said bagger was willing to walk her to her car.

She was rethinking her independent streak a few seconds later as she tried to push the cart with the groceries and boxes.

She got the groceries into the back of the station wagon but was in the process of turning around to get her boxes when a little gust of wind took her cart away.

"Shoot!" She watched it roll off.

It was headed toward the fancy SUV that was parked in the parking space across the lot. The boxes fell out all over the place as her cart picked up speed and headed directly toward what had to be the nicest car in Lenawee County.

Of course.

J.J. ran after her wayward cart. But it was too late. She lunged forward to try to stop the collision, but didn't make it in time.

The Irish Hills Village Market Cart hit the sleek black Range Rover, square on the side panel, and then, for good measure, scraped forward toward the driver's door.

J.J. grabbed it and prayed to the gods of grocery carts that this wasn't a several-thousand-dollar situation.

She backed up a step, looked at the car panel...and then the door opened.

It made her jump back; she hadn't realized the car was occupied.

A pair of expensive-looking leather loafers stepped out, attached to a pair of too-new jeans. Her eyes traveled up, and then she realized whom she'd hit.

Stone Stirling appeared, and J.J. looked into the ice-blue eyes of her arch-enemy.

And unfortunately, she had to apologize to him.

She took a breath and took her medicine.

"I'm sorry, Mr. Stirling, the cart got away from me."

He looked at the car, now sporting a long scratch from bumper to door. "It's okay."

"I'm going to pay for it. Ugh, I know a guy at Adrian Auto Body. Probably can buff it out for you."

Stone raised an eyebrow at her. "It's okay, J.J., really."

"What, you've got three more just like it in the fleet back at your underground lair?" J.J. couldn't help it; sometimes the snark just came out.

"How did you guess?"

This exchange had lasted longer than she had time or desire for it to last. *Time to wrap this up.*

"Well, if you change your mind, just let me know, and I'll take a second job or sell my future grandchildren or whatever to pay for it." She figured the SUV cost more than her first house and car. Maybe all the houses on her block combined.

Stone Stirling laughed and shook his head.

Why was he being nice? Whatever, she had half a dozen boxes to collect that littered the parking lot; she didn't have time to puzzle out his game. She yanked the cart back and slid it into the cart return.

"Can I help?"

J.J. was struggling to chase the boxes now that the wind had picked up, and they were sliding away from her in all directions, albeit slowly. Her face was flushed with embarrassment. She'd turned into a gawky teenager out of nowhere.

"No, no, I'm fine," she said as she bent down for a box that had slipped away. She felt like she was suddenly in a silent movie comedy, and she was the clown.

Despite her protest, the billionaire started chasing the boxes, too.

"I said I could do it myself." But she was losing the battle.

Finally, after several comical minutes, J.J. had loaded two boxes into the back of her vintage Ford Escort Station Wagon, and Stone Stirling was behind her with four more.

"Here, you go." He slid them in, and she was forced to be polite and grateful.

"Thank you."

"Are you moving so soon after getting back?"

How did he know I had gone? She was reasonably sure he only knew she existed because she'd told him off on behalf of Libby, any chance she got.

"Did you miss me? I know I'm one of your favorite townies."

"I did. And you are."

"Right. Yeah, okay, so I'm out of here. Thanks for the help. And let me know if I owe you for the door."

J.J. did not like a helpful or friendly Stone Stirling. She was still in battle mode against the guy, even though she hadn't seen him in months, and they'd beat him at his own game.

She left him in the parking lot.

If she had to pay for his car, it would not be cheap. All that work to get the free boxes, and she mangles Stone Stirling's car in the process. *Typical!*

J.J. tried to shake off the encounter and focus on something else.

Getting to Nora House, a bottle of wine, and some good cheese was the order of the rest of the night. She needed to rest and regroup so she could box D.J. on the ears tomorrow and face off against whatever BS he was into.

Chapter Six

"Surprise!"

Goldie ran out of Nora House and straight for her.

"Oh, I would have bought more wine if I'd known!"

Goldie hugged her tightly. "No worries. I raided the cellar at the restaurant."

Hope was right behind Goldie. And another hug came her way. "Let us help you carry stuff inside."

As they did, it was Viv's turn to burst out of Nora House.

Viv! She was stunning, glowing, healthy!

"You look so beautiful, so beautiful!" J.J. said and meant it.

The last time she'd seen Viv, her old friend was fresh off the battle for her life. Now, she looked like the embodiment of the spring blossoms that were bursting out all over the place.

J.J. felt a pang of guilt. She'd vowed to be there for Viv during her cancer recovery. They all had. But J.J. had bailed. She'd run. But she still didn't see any other way after the tornado.

The scrum of Sandbar Sisters made their way inside Nora House. This place was her sanctuary as a kid; more home than home sometimes. And even now, J.J. felt instantly at home here.

As they walked through the mudroom entry, past the kitchen,

and toward the open family room, J.J. was pleased to see Libby hadn't modernized or updated yet. There was new paint and some new touches from Libby throughout the house, but much of it was the same, with Emma's vibe still permeating the space. Nora House was *actually* vintage, not faux vintage. It appeared that as much as Libby had worked to restore things, build things, and bolster Irish Hills, she also knew it was the history of the place that gave it its heart.

Nora House was, in some ways, just as much hers as it was Libby's.

She thought she'd be safe from memories of Dean here. How could she have forgotten the best one?

1996

The day was a little overcast. J.J. was nervous, not that it would rain, but that Jackie would say something offensive, or Jared would knock a beer over on the delicate upholstery.

Why did I agree to this?

Nora House had been her solace as a kid, back when she imagined that nothing less than a member of Duran Duran was husband material.

It was an accident, really, that this had come to be. Aunt Emma had her head in J.J.'s shampoo bowl, and she saw it.

"Is that an engagement ring?"

Emma had sat up, water dripping everywhere, and grabbed J.J.'s soapy hand.

"It is," J.J. told her. "I mean, it's not up to your level of jewelry, but yeah."

"Nonsense!" Aunt Emma said as she hugged her.

"Sit back down. You're getting water everywhere."

J.J. had just gotten her cosmetology license, but Shelly still had her washing everyone's hair like she'd started yesterday. Two years of driving an hour down to the Toledo School of Beauty and she was still fighting Shelly for her own clients.

Aunt Emma was one of those clients, but this little power play by Shelly had turned out to be a surprise gift for J.J.

By the time Shelly had set Aunt Emma's bouffant, J.J. had a wedding venue fit for old money.

Emma insisted on Nora House, buying a dress for J.J., and getting Reverend Alden to come to the house to perform the ceremony.

At first, it seemed like a dream come true, but now that the big day had arrived, J.J. was concerned. *What if Dean's friend Moose sits in an antique chair and busts it? Will this be way too fancy?*

The house was buzzing with activity. Aunt Emma had insisted not only on throwing J.J.'s wedding and reception, but also on getting the food and drinks. There was a staff of people putting together a buffet that would be assembled out on the back porch after she and Dean said their vows.

Luckily, the guest list was impromptu and small. The original plan had been to go to the courthouse and be done with it. There wasn't time for save the date cards or a regiment of Princess Diana-inspired bridesmaids. Still, it was a more significant affair than J.J. had ever imagined, aside from her fantasy wedding to Duran Duran bassist John Taylor, of course.

When the time came to tie the knot, J.J. had two "bridesmaids," her brother Jared and her mom, Jackie.

J.J. put her arm through Jackie's and Jared's, and the three of them walked with her from the grand sitting room out to the porch and down the walkway toward the lake.

At the end of the walk was Dean. Moose stood next to him. Both were sweating like it was their job. A smattering of two dozen or so other guests sat in white wooden folding chairs, including Dean's parents, his construction crew, and J.J.'s friends from beauty school. She counted thirty people or so, ten times more than she'd have had at the courthouse.

Dean's crew had rolled a keg onto the back porch, and J.J. had nearly cussed them all out about it. But Aunt Emma told her to hush. She said, as the bride, J.J. had two jobs.

"Just get down the aisle looking pretty. That's easy for you, sweetheart, but then try to lock the memories into your head. It's not going to be easy. It's going to be a blur. I'll handle the rest. Though I will say that keg better not be something stupid, like Pabst Blue Ribbon."

Emma, the beer expert! Who knew?

The lake was beautiful. The midday sun had burned off the morning's overcast skies. The sun's rays dappled the little waves on Lake Manitou with twinkling lights. The sun could also be blamed for her sweating groom and his red-faced best man. J.J. decided their impromptu bachelor party could also be blamed, so she did not feel bad about their slight discomfort.

Serves them right if I have to wear these heels!

Reverend Alden had done a million weddings, and he, too, was likely getting a little warm in the sun. There had been no rehearsal. All J.J. wanted was to keep it short. She suspected Dean would sweat through the suit jacket if it went on too long. And she wasn't one for hearts and flowers, either. Keep it short. That was the only thing she'd really told Reverend Alden.

She knew she was in love with Dean. Because of that, she'd decided to give marriage a go. Even though she didn't have an actual example of how marriage worked. She was worried about that, but it was too late now. They were in this thing.

Over Dean's shoulder, J.J. saw the family of swans swim by, upstaging the bride with their icy-white plumage, she feared.

J. J. barely heard the words the preacher said. But she did look at Dean. His gaze was steady, even though his forehead was sweaty. His strong presence reminded her why she had decided to do this.

He was why she'd said yes. Not some delusion that she was getting a picket fence.

She nearly called it off a dozen times. But J.J. knew a good catch when she saw one, whether it was a friend or a boyfriend. Dean Tucker might be rough around the edges, but he was solid as a rock, and he was in love with her. He put her first in a way no one else had ever done. And he was tough. She'd thrown barbs at him, pretended she wasn't interested, and had tested him. It didn't faze him.

So, here she was, on the lawn of Nora House, Lake Manitou sparkling behind them and Moose, behind her Dean, looking more nervous than all the rest of them.

That was it, her Dean.

"Now, if the bride and groom have prepared a few words?"

"What?" J.J. had sort of zoned out, but that snapped her back.

"You have a moment to exchange your personal vows."

"We don't have that; we didn't do that." She felt a bit panicked. Everyone was looking, and she was about to trip at the finish line of this ceremony.

"I did, so I'll do mine, okay?"

Dean wrote vows? Oh, boy, buckle up. What was this going to be?

Dean squeezed her hands, then let one go to fish a piece of paper out of his sport coat pocket.

He cleared his throat and then spoke. No stutter, no mumbling. His voice was better than the preacher who did this for a living.

"J.J., I want to promise you a few really big things in front of everyone."

J.J. had no idea what he was going to say. But Dean did. He looked taller than she'd ever seen him, more handsome, and somehow also vulnerable.

"I will always take care of you. I will work hard. I will put you first, before Moose and them. I know I'm the luckiest man on Earth, that Len at the Michigan Tavern has no idea what a real I.D.

looks like and let you in with that ridiculous one you had. I promise I'll never forget that. I can't promise I won't break the furniture. Ask Mom; it happens more than you'd guess, but I do promise to try not to—and to fix whatever I might smash. Also, I love you. I maybe should have said that first."

It took her by surprise; it swept her off her feet. Anyone who knew her knew J.J. was a talker. But the words didn't come. Instead, tears came. A lot of them. Dean reached across and wiped a few.

"I'm the lucky one," was all she could think of to say. She didn't even say she loved him, too. Her emotions wiped all sense of what to say out of her head.

She wished she had said she loved him too.

He'd declared that she had his heart in her hands, and in that moment, she knew, too, that he had hers.

"You may kiss the bride!"

They did just that. And she heard Jackie cackle and clap. It didn't annoy her as it might any other time.

J.J. stepped back. She put her hand in his. He'd said all the right things.

She'd tripped over her words, and later, when they were enjoying the lovely buffet Aunt Emma had arranged, she leaned her head on Dean's shoulder.

"I should have said more and that I love you. Back there with the vows."

"You talk plenty," Dean replied.

And that was the start of it, her wedding day.

Chapter Seven

Present Day

It came rushing back to her. It was a swell. It lifted her up and then washed over her head. J.J. had thought she was going to get away from Dean's memory if she stayed here instead of the house, and yet, there it was. *How could I have forgotten about the most important day I had here?*

None of her Sandbar Sisters were at her wedding. They'd completely lost touch by that point. Maybe that was it. Maybe that was why she'd forgotten.

Or had I just pushed the memory down, replaced by thousands of other less special days that had made up our lives together?

"Honey, are you okay?"

Viv was next to her. She'd stopped cold. She'd been gripped by it. Her friends stopped what they were doing, too.

She hadn't been taking these moments out and living with them. She'd blocked them all. And then here, out of the blue, she was under the water of her grief.

"I really sucked at wedding vows," J.J. said by way of explanation. Her throat hurt like it was closing. Her fists were in tight balls. "I didn't tell Dean I loved him when we got married here. Right here." She put a hand to her lips and pressed hard, like she was going to keep something inside her body.

"You need to let this go. It's us," Goldie said.

"I'm trying to hold—" but J.J. didn't get the words out. She cried. It probably sounded more like a wounded animal. But she didn't care. For the first time, she didn't care. She let the tears come and the feelings she'd been so terrified of.

Viv held her. Goldie had a hand on one shoulder, Hope the other. Libby put a hand on her head. But they didn't say anything. They were there, in the swell with her. They were there if the water was too rough. If she stopped trying to tread water, to fight the waves, they were there to pull her up into the raft.

That's what it felt like.

She'd avoided this moment and closed the door to her emotions. That was the whole reason she came to Nora House. And now it was out, in all its rough edges and racking sobs.

And then it ebbed. She could swallow. Breath. She could see.

"Okay, wow. Okay." The flow of tears stopped. Her head throbbed a little.

"I think we need to sit out by the water, yeah?" Libby said.

She was right. The lake was their place. The best place.

"I've got nowhere to be but here," Goldie said.

That was the international movie star telling her this was more important than any other thing.

"Really? I've got a red carpet somewhere," J.J. said.

Goldie laughed, and the group of them started gathering their supplies for a nice sit by the lake.

It was a little too early to be in bathing suits and lying on their beloved raft. But it was the perfect day for the Adirondack chairs.

The sun warmed. It didn't burn.

"So, you didn't tell us about your wedding to Dean. I actually had no idea that you did it here," Libby said.

"I sort of forgot. Great wife, eh?"

"No, it's just lovely. I'm glad you did."

"And I heard you tell Dean you loved him multiple times. It was rather sickening," Hope pointed out, handing her a fresh glass of wine.

"Ha, yeah, I guess. I just meant during our vows. I really blew it."

"Wedding vows are overrated. It's the day-to-day that counts. If my ex had said, 'Hi, I'm gay, but I love you, and we're going to have a great life,' I might have been better equipped," Viv said.

"True, Bret was a good husband, other than that," Goldie added.

They spent the evening watching the water, laughing, and drinking wine. J.J. had let out something she'd been holding in. She'd faced something she'd been afraid of.

The tears terrified her, but shedding them today had helped. Her friends had helped.

Maybe being back in Irish Hills is okay. Maybe I'll be able to do what I need to do without feeling awful.

Or maybe not. She had no roadmap for the trip she was on now. But there was a lot of comfort in her friends and the town that she loved.

Maybe I can be here without Dean, at least for a little while.

Chapter Eight

J.J.'s day was going to start with D.J. She'd had a lovely time with her Sandbar Sisters. They'd offered a million different ways to help her and then did what she asked and stopped fussing.

She was not a fan of being fussed over.

They had given her love, support, and Nora House to land, and they'd given her wine and good laughs last night.

She knew she didn't want to stay at Nora House, though. She had faced the memory of the wedding day and had a nice night's sleep, but being here wasn't much better than her own house.

She didn't want to be at Nora House or her house with Dean. *Where did that leave her?* J.J. would have to tackle that later.

Right now, it was time to deal with D.J.

Libby was up and out early, doing what Libby does, which is to say, everything. Her friend had left a note and then left her to deal with her son.

J.J. headed to the construction trailer, wondering if dealing with D.J. would be like dealing with Dean back in their early days.

J.J. wasn't worried about the trailer stirring up grief or memory. It was a relatively new development in Dean's contracting business, the trailer. It had become a necessity after

Dean's business had boomed, thanks to the expansion of Irish Hills and Libby's ongoing downtown renovations. That he had an "office" other than the front seat of his truck or the corner of the kitchen at their house was, to them, a huge milestone. They were practically moguls! That's what they'd joked about. Watch out, world: Tucker Construction has an office trailer!

When Dean first started in construction, he did anything for anyone. There was no job too small. Someone needed a deck. He built a deck; a roof, he'd be there; a fence, he'd install it. Dean would take any job he could.

Irish Hills is small, and he was a kid back then, really. He'd gone from high school construction trade classes and what he learned from his dad to taking jobs.

A couple years out of high school, Dean earned an associate degree in construction tech. He'd just finished it when he met J.J.

He'd also just bought his first truck back then.

J.J. was so proud of Dean, how he'd built everything with his own two hands.

She drove downtown. The trailer had a semi-permanent space these days behind the row of buildings that were under various states of renovation. She loved that D.J. was trying to fill his dad's Carhartt, but it sounded like the two men had more in common than she'd understood when she left on her "North American Grief Avoidance Tour."

J.J. pulled up to the trailer. The logo for Dean Tucker Construction had been designed and painted onto the trailer right before the tornado. J.J. had been encouraging Dean to put some signage on his stuff. She thought it was good advertising. Dean pushed back on the idea.

"I don't need to advertise. I've got more work than we can get to right now," Dean had said.

"You never know," had been her reply.

He took almost every suggestion she offered when it came to ideas for expanding Tucker Construction. She thought a logo and a phone number display was a good idea because you never do know.

I guess I was right about that.

J.J. walked up to the door and knocked. She stepped back as the door swung open, and D.J. leaned out; he had a phone to his ear.

"I told you I'll be there after I get off the phone with the inspector."

J.J. cocked her head; it was still hard to believe how grown her boys were. One day, they went down to the basement to play with Pokémon cards, and she swore they walked back up those stairs two minutes later looking like their mountain man dad.

"Mom! Oh, no, uh, yes, sorry, for sure. I'll be there for sure." D.J. held up his index finger to let her know, one second. She nodded. He stepped back into the trailer, and she stepped up into it.

"No, no, I know, so sorry, just wires crossed, and it's all good. Promise."

D.J. finished the call.

"Momma!" He wrapped J.J. in a hug, and she squeezed tight. It had been nine months; could a grown man grow more? If so, D.J. had added size in all directions.

"Good to see you, sweetie, and good to see you hard at work."

D.J. immediately got a little sheepish.

Well, he wasn't shameless, at least.

"Have a seat, here, here." He picked up his laptop from the little bench mounted to the trailer wall surrounding the table. J.J. had no doubt neither the father nor son could actually sit on the bench. The size of them would surely rip out the wall anchors.

"Some news, the house is sold."

"Grandma Jackie okay with that?"

Despite moving years ago, Jackie still called Irish Hills her summer home. She "wintered" in Winter Park.

"Not her call." J.J., truth be told, hadn't thought much about her mom's lifestyle in the last few months. She didn't have it in her to nurture anyone, even herself, after Dean.

"Well, it is her summer crash pad."

"True, one issue at a time, I guess." She'd deal with Jackie when she had to.

"Selling the house is why you're back?"

"Partly. I bet you can guess the other part."

D.J. shook his head and looked down.

"Mom, I told Libby it wouldn't happen again. It was Chris Loger's bachelor party. You know how that goes. He's a maniac. Got out of hand."

"Chris is getting married, that's nice. To whom?"

"Girl he met over in Onsted. She does blood draws…what's that called?"

"Phlebotomist."

"Yeah, that, over at Bixby."

"Hmm, well, the fact remains you were three sheets to the wind on the job or not on the job."

"I know, I know. It was so stupid. Loger got Everclear, and I thought it was vodka, and Everclear is brutal, just brutal. Anyway, I'd worked all day, all week, and no sleep and just bad combo."

J.J. did know Everclear was potent. She also knew that even when you were "the boss" of this operation, it was back-breaking labor in between dozens of logistical nightmares. She worried again about the level of responsibility her boy had undertaken with all this.

"That stuff is brutal, no doubt."

"I'm a beer guy, you know that."

"You promise you're okay?"

"I'm mad as heck at Loger. He really messed us all up. You should have seen Reggie Barton; he was sick as a dog."

J.J. rolled her eyes. "I can picture it, thanks."

"Okay, so we're cool. You don't need to worry."

"I'll always worry. That's what I do."

"Mom, stop, it's fine."

D.J. did seem fine, and she never liked that Loger kid anyway. It was no surprise that D.J. got blackout drunk at something the Loger kid planned. Once upon a time, he'd encouraged her youngest, Austin, to jump off the roof into an above-ground pool. She still shuddered to think about what could have happened. What *had* happened was Austin caught his foot on the edge and wound up with fifteen stitches from ankle to knee. That Loger kid was still a lousy influence, apparently.

"Okay, okay. Are you sure this isn't too much, too soon? You still had a lot to learn from Dad."

"I learned. I promise."

"What about Austin? Is he helping? You know he's ready to help."

"I don't want to bug him. He's busy with his classes."

Austin was in construction trades at the community college, just like his dad.

"Well, this would seem like the perfect job for that coursework." She'd talk to Austin herself. Maybe he was too busy to pitch in like she'd hoped.

D.J.'s phone buzzed.

"Ugh, the tile guy, calling me back. Libby wants to see one wall pretty much done before she commits."

She had said her piece. Hopefully, that was all the situation required, a reminder that people were counting on Tucker Construction. "I'll get out of your hair. You're busy. Dinner this week, and maybe also I cut your hair?"

D.J.'s hair was grazing his shoulders. She reached out to the curls that dusted his collar. The same ones that used to peak out of a football helmet and further back lay against his neck when he was in his crib.

What the heck is wrong with me? All these darn memories, everywhere I go!

"Yes, it's definitely a deal, food and a haircut."

"Okay, get back to work. Don't make Libby mad. It's terrifying."

"Oh, I know, I know."

She wondered if there were other incidents she didn't know about. *Had Libby overreacted, or had she been pushed to the limit?*

D.J. hugged her again. As she left, he was on the phone, sounding professional, busy, and responsible.

It's okay, Tucker Construction is okay, and D.J. just made a mistake. It happens.

J.J. was relieved there wasn't more to it. The trailer was a little messy and disorganized, but that was her mom brain trying to control things. The boys were a mess a lot of the time.

She also figured Libby had never seen the rough and tumble side of Irish Hills. It wasn't her experience, and she'd likely never had a contractor sleep it off in front of her. She was a silver spoon in a blue-collar situation. That was it.

That was also understandable. Libby had a lot on her plate, and D.J. had dropped the ball.

But in J.J.'s estimation, things were back on track.

That was one less thing to worry about. *Thank goodness.*

Chapter Nine

Libby

She had J.J. back. It wasn't how she would have planned to have to do it. But the result was that J.J. was back in town, and hopefully, that also meant D.J. was on the right path.

She didn't have the time—or truth be told, the money—to find a new contractor to finish what needed finishing in downtown Irish Hills.

She was lucky. Granite Insurance had paid out initially when the tornado ripped through last summer.

But there weren't any extra funds. The time lost, and the expense of finding a new firm to take over the project, would set them back too far. She'd never get the places leased if she had to restart with a new contractor. Still, there were a lot of loose ends; with D.J., more loose ends than tied in the last few weeks.

Libby looked at the books for the redevelopment project. It was a razor's edge between staying afloat and sinking to the bottom of Lake Manitou. She never felt done or even safe. If it wasn't one thing, it was another. She knew she thrived under this type of pressure; she'd faced worse odds. Now that J.J. was back, that would tip the balance back in the right direction.

Today's meeting was vital. She was meeting with Granite Insurance to convince them to continue coverage of her disaster-prone redevelopment.

The value of the project was always future value. Granite took a considerable risk in covering the buildings, and then, of course, they had to pay out, thanks to the tornado.

The renovations had taken longer than she'd hoped, so the costs were going up, and the potential income going down.

That damn tornado. It was so capricious and random, and yet twice in the town's life, Mother Nature had chosen to unleash her wrath on Irish Hills.

When Libby was young, it hurt the town. It changed the course of the town's life but not her life. No one she knew died. Sure, a lot of destruction happened, but it wasn't her heart. It wasn't her future. Her future was in the big city with Henry. Her plans were away, not here.

But this time, the storm hit her in all ways. All worse. All awful.

The town had survived, in some ways, much better this time than the twister of their youth. But her heart, all of their hearts, were swept into despair unlike anything they'd ever known. Dean Tucker was important to J.J., for sure, to their boys, but also to Libby. That evil tornado had taken a bedrock from all of them.

The loss of Dean could also prove to be the loss of all they'd worked for. Libby used this as fuel. She'd win again, and it was going to be for Dean just as much as for Irish Hills.

Libby loved D.J. She wanted him to rise to the occasion. It was easy to forget he wasn't Dean. He was still young. Dean was so good at his job, and Libby had grown to rely on him. They'd had a language between them for how to complete a project. It wasn't fair to put any of that on D.J. She had to remember that she was training D.J., in many ways, helping him learn what she needed.

But the drinking, that was another kettle of fish.

D.J. had a problem, and he needed help. Thank goodness J.J. was back to take the reins.

Hopefully, that was a problem managed, and she could confidently tell the reps from Granite Insurance that they were on track, close to getting tenants in, and worthy of full coverage.

She'd spoken to the reps on the phone, back when she was searching for insurance before the tornado and again after it hit. They were based in New York and decided to come visit. She'd hoped D.J. would have finished the one whole unit before their arrival, but that hadn't happened.

Libby was nervous. She needed to convince them that this town was a good bet. Continuing to insure Libby's projects was smart business. Since the project wasn't where she wanted it to be, she'd take the reps to see her success stories instead.

Siena's store was a hot spot, and people came from all over the state to see her unique take on home décor. The Mercantile was hopping, and of course, Hope's place barely ever had an empty table. Libby had also just signed a lease for a quirky new bookstore to open in the space between the mercantile and the restaurant.

There was only one vacant spot left. She knew the lakeside of the street rehabilitation was an unqualified success.

Libby's office, when she wasn't working from Nora House, was in the final vacant space. She'd swept the floor, alerted the rest of the tenants that they were getting a visit from the insurance bigwigs, and set coffee and muffins out.

She was ready to go to bat for Irish Hills again.

The door opened precisely at 9 a.m., and in walked the suit. It was an expensive suit. She didn't know if that was good or bad. Her eyes traveled from loafers to necktie, and then the jury was in. It was bad.

The suit in question was none other than Stone Stirling.

They'd come a long way in nine months, given that she'd tried to punch him out back then. And he'd done an amazing job with the grocery store, admittedly. He clearly felt they'd come a long way, too, or he'd have his hands up, ready to deflect an attack.

"I'm sorry, Stone. I have an important meeting about to start. Can you come back another time, or text me, or better yet, none of the above." She may not want to punch the guy in the face anymore, but she also wasn't going to roll out the red carpet.

"I'm honored."

"What?"

"That you consider a meeting with me important, it touches me to my core."

He was in her way, just trying to needle her. She didn't want to be on edge when the insurance people got here. She wanted to be on her game.

"Stone, seriously, can you just? I have bigger fish to fry."

"There can't possibly be a bigger fish. Do you even read *Forbes*?"

"What, what can I do for you?"

"It's what I can do for *you* if I feel it makes good sense."

"I really can't right now." Libby looked behind Stone, around one of his impossibly square shoulders.

"Relax, *I'm* your meeting."

"What?" Libby stared at Stone. There was a little smirk on his face.

"I thought the name gave it away, actually," Stone said, shrugging.

"Wait, Granite Insurance? Stone, *you're* Granite?"

"That sentence sounds ridiculous, but I am."

Libby took a step backward and then began to pace. Stone was behind the insurance company that they'd been using! He was the one who'd paid out after the tornado. He was the one who she was hoping to convince to keep insuring downtown Irish Hills.

"Did you make it impossible for legitimate insurance companies to take our business? That's unethical, that's underhanded. That's exactly what I should have expected from you."

Stone raised his hands up; he did remember her temper from last year. "Hang on, hang on. No. You are a huge risk. This project is a huge risk. You got rejected by all the big companies all on your own. I had nothing whatsoever to do with that."

"Then how?"

"I just happened to invest in a firm specializing in high-risk development projects. I thought I'd need it over in Covert Pier. But they got standard rates and coverage. You found Granite, not the other way around."

Libby had beaten out Covert Pier in the competition for a development grant. Stone had tried to tilt the playing field against her by investing in that resort town while trying to take over Irish Hills for a stupid gas station.

She thought she'd won, but maybe that was all an illusion.

But what Stone said about the insurance was true. When they couldn't get coverage, Libby had called every single firm in the country, and found Granite was willing to take a chance. They were the only ones willing to, and now she knew why.

"You did everything you could to beat us and couldn't, and now, what? We're not insured? You're going to put a road block up for our projects, so I can't go elsewhere. Admit it! Whatever it is, I'll figure it out. It's you who is no match for me!"

"I agree. One hundred percent."

"So, what are you after? What's the play?"

"I'm just looking to rent this very space we're in, your last unleased spot on this side, right?"

"What? You've got the grocery store, and now you want this space? Am I hearing this right?"

"Yes, actually, you get this strip fully occupied and profitable. You can probably get any insurance company to take a chance on you after the contract is up. You'll be off my hands. Or rather, off Granite's books."

"What's your angle?"

"No angle. I actually like not being at odds with you. Granite will be your insurance provider until such time as you're a better risk. I'll help you be a better risk by finishing this side of the street off. Fully occupied, all profitable—the sky's the limit across the street if this is the model."

Libby was trying to think like Stone Stirling. He'd failed at taking over Irish Hills and bulldozing it to turn it into a highway exit. Now, he seemed to be trying to take over in a whole new way from the inside out.

"I'm perfectly able to find a tenant."

"Right, yet here it sits, vacant. And as confident as you seem to be, one tenant is your friend who's a restauranteur, and another is your daughter's friend who is a home décor shop owner. You seem to be running out of friends. If you could have rented this space, you would have."

"How is me tapping into my network to get businesses off the ground any different from you tapping into yours?"

"Hmm, no different, really, no criticism."

"What, you're going to put a turkey of a business in here, bring down the whole block?"

"That's ridiculous. I like making money, not losing it."

"I still cannot figure you out."

"Let me take this lease. You have full occupancy, your projects look more attractive, and you won't even need Granite Insurance next year when the insurance issue comes up again."

"And if I say no?"

"You say no, but you know, Granite's contract is up, and what if, say, the executives there don't want to renew, based on the fact that this place isn't complete, and the repairs are wildly behind schedule and over budget across the street?"

"You just said you're Granite." Libby was furious; he'd beat her, and she hadn't even seen it coming.

"Oops, yes, I guess I am. Can I tell you the truth?"

"I don't know. I think this is some sort of long game way to do what you always wanted here, take over Irish Hills and turn into, ugh, I have no idea."

"I'm not sure how many things I need to say and do to convince you I'm on your side now. I want Irish Hills to succeed. The truth is, I like this place. Sure, I want to own a business or two, but be hands on. I want to be in this as a community member. Not someone who choppers in and out."

"You sound sincere, but why do I feel like you're trapping me in some flipping spider web?"

"You're very dramatic. There's no trap, no web, just a guy standing in front of a community developer asking her to lease him a retail space."

"Ha, ha." She couldn't help but laugh. She turned so he wouldn't see her actually break. He did seem sincere. But she needed her game face.

"Okay, here's the condition. I decide what goes in here."

"What?"

"Yeah, so you don't put a clunker in here that brings down the block. I can see you putting in a dollar store or a dispensary."

"You're acting like I run vape stores and strip clubs."

She knew he didn't, but what if that was the play? She agrees to let him take this space, and he intentionally ruins it? *No way!*

"Well, what do you have in mind? You haven't said."

"Actually, I don't know. I was just hoping, believe it or not, to help you get this project finished. Maybe one national chain here, something that's tasteful, a little cutting edge? That wouldn't be the worst thing for this town."

Libby wasn't against big chains, but she didn't like it for downtown. She wanted to keep the local and unique feel here as much as possible. Her mind raced over what would work for the last spot on this stretch of shops.

And then it hit her, a way to keep an eye on Stone and keep her friend in town, at least for a little bit.

"We need a salon."

"What?"

"A salon. Since Hairdo or Dye went under. We need a salon."

"Great, fine. A salon. I'll lease this space and get a salon in here."

"And you'll hire J.J."

"What?"

"I said, you'll hire J.J. to consult. If there's one thing she knows, it's the hairdo needs of Irish Hills. I want her on your team."

"Sure, whatever. I really do want to help. I want to make sure the town thrives; I promise you that."

"Yeah, sure, but this the only way I can be certain you're not trying to sabotage our progress. She won't let you." *This idea is brilliant. This is it!*

"You're paranoid."

"If I was paranoid, I would have looked into Granite a heck of a lot more than I did."

"Fine, it's a deal. I'll sign the lease of this building and get Irish Hills a beauty salon." Stone Stirling was shaking his head as though the idea was absurd.

"And J.J. will be your consultant, so it's not crap."

"As you wish."

Aha! I've got him again!

They shook hands, and Libby realized, as she looked into the confident eyes of Stone Stirling, that actually *she* had acquiesced to everything *he'd* asked for. She'd won nothing.

And Libby now had to convince J.J. to keep an eye on the snake she had accidentally let in. That might not be easy.

But J.J. was tougher than any billionaire and just as stubborn.

Chapter Ten

J.J.

What would be the hardest thing to pack up? What would be the most gut-wrenching? J.J. decided to tackle the worst first.

She'd already moved on in her life in terms of little kid stuff. Dean and she had already empty nested. Over the last few years, they had begun to fix up the house for adults, not toddlers or teens. They envisioned transitioning this family home into the perfect place for two.

She had a box of baby things and mementos already in storage. She'd done that when she eyed their rooms and cleaned the basement. There were a few things that the boys could have if they ever settled down and had kids. She had scrapbooks, but she had Swedish Death Cleaned the rest.

She'd ruthlessly garage saled or donated a toy chest full of swords, light sabers, and ball bats. The truth was that D.J. and Austin were hard on physical objects. Most of the stuff she cleaned out after they left home was already busted. Having a tidy place for the first time in her life did not fill her with sadness. She didn't need to hang on to old purses or shoes. The idea that her own sons would have to paw through dozens of pieces of flotsam after she shook off her mortal coil gave her anxiety.

A few boxes of things that were sweet or precious were all she kept. No more than half a dozen. This gift of decluttering was one she'd give to her sons when they were grieving again. Someday, they would appreciate this economy instead of cursing the chore of having to clean up after her life.

Or not. Who knew what sons really understood about their mothers anyway?

So, the worst first thing? It was Dean's clothes. She'd never opened the closet after he died. Didn't look at it. Touch it. Smell it. Nothing. But now, she had to. She walked through the small hallway into their room and stared at the closed closet door. She stopped thinking about what she'd find and just decided to dive in. She'd let it smack her in the face. It would sting. But it had to be done.

J.J. pushed open the closet she'd allowed him to have. It was a sliver, he'd joked, compared to what she had.

"I'm a bear of a human, and I have six square inches of closet space. You're the size of a Keebler Elf, and you've got our bedroom, and now you need the spare room closet, too?"

"Correct."

Dean complained, but then he installed a cedar closet liner for her.

J.J. looked at the neatly stacked jeans. She ran her hand over the dozen flannels hung by her over a year ago now. She'd already given all of Dean's heavy coats and workwear to the boys. They could pack them, unpack them, donate them, or do whatever they needed to do. This was different. These were the day-to-day things of his life.

She knew what Dean would say about all this. It was just stuff. Clothes did not make the man. But looking at Dean's clothes, she could see all the man had made. These were the garments of the hard-working, unpretentious, loyal, and sometimes genius, in her mind, man that was Dean Tucker. Flannel, denim, corduroy, cotton, and wool. Not a fine fabric in the mix. Everything was tough but also soft with wear and in good shape because he cared.

J.J. saw Dean as clear as day, standing with her.

"Pack 'em up. They're just collecting dust. There's a young kid out there who needs some of these duds."

And he was right. J.J. grabbed as many shirts as she could in one bundle and put them in the box she'd lugged in. The jeans went in next. She was about to tape it shut—it was best to be fast—when one item caught her eye.

"That son of a gun," she said out loud.

The oldest flannel, the one he'd told her he'd thrown out, was buried in the middle of the newer ones she'd diligently acquired for him over more recent years.

J.J. picked it out of the lot.

"Well, you survived me twice. Dean saved you, eh? Fine."

J.J. had a pile on the kitchen table, stuff to keep. Photo albums, the fancy silver from Dean's grandma, and now, this one flannel. Buffalo plaid, for goodness' sake; he always looked like young Santa in it. The flannel that irritated her the most was the one she wouldn't part with.

"You win on this old thing, Dean. You win."

She'd have the boys go through the shed out back, grab any tools they still wanted, and that was it.

Dean didn't make furniture or collectible crafts. He built decks, roofs, room additions, and staircases. She couldn't pack that up. She couldn't give the boys some chest of drawers he carved or a table he'd turned.

But Dean's work was all over the county. J.J. took comfort in that.

The rest of the stuff was in the garage. She'd have Goodwill come get it.

A couple of hours of work had reduced a couple of decades of life into the pile on the kitchen table.

She was at once relieved that she'd made it through this job and also slightly panicked. If there was nothing to do anymore as Mrs. Dean Tucker, was she still Mrs. Dean Tucker?

J.J. shook it off. *Dean wouldn't want me to be wallowing, and I'm not going to, darn it. That kind of thinking won't get me anywhere.*

A knock at the door was well-timed to interrupt the flow of tears that was sure to follow if she kept standing in the house and reminiscing.

J.J. opened the door to find Libby looking strange, and next to her, Stone Stirling, in full Stone Stirling billionaire business attire.

"Uh, hi?"

"We need to talk to you."

"Look, if this is about your Range Rover, I said I'd pay for it. But I want a local estimate. I'm not doing some jacked-up East Coast repair fee. In fact, I may try to buff it out myself. We all don't have a billion dollars sitting around. And getting Libby involved? That's just, I don't even know what." Her melancholy had swiftly moved over for a fiery dose of outrage.

"What are you talking about?" Libby looked confused.

"His car, my cart hit his car. And to be honest, I'm not even sure if I am liable for that, but even so, I'll pay."

Stone Stirling was smiling.

Why was he smiling?

"Can we come in?"

"Yes, sure."

J.J. stepped back, and Libby and Stone were now in her cozy family room. She wondered when the last time the billionaire had been in a room this small, if ever.

"I'm not here about the car. It's not your problem, truly," Stone said.

"I'm not asking for charity; I'm just saying I'm not buying an entire new quarter panel for your jacked-up SUV."

"J.J., stop," Libby said. "We've got something to talk to you about."

"Not the scratch?"

"Not the scratch," Libby confirmed.

"What then?"

"I'd like to hire you to consult on my new project," Stone said.

"Well, I'd like you to kiss my—"

"J.J.," Libby interjected and put her hand up.

"What? Is he nuts?" J.J. directed this at Libby, who shook her head "no."

"He's not. It's a great opportunity. Just hear us out."

J.J. narrowed her eyes.

"I need an expert," Stone added, "and you're the expert."

Chapter Eleven

J.J.

"I want you to take the lead in setting up my new venture," Stone continued. "The salon will take the remaining spot in the north side of Irish Hills downtown."

"You're the best person for this," Libby added. "You know the local clientele, and you're on the pulse of what they do in Ann Arbor and the bigger places. My hair hasn't looked right since you left."

"That much is true," J.J. quipped. Her friend was talking fast, though, barely letting her get a word in edgewise. This was a sure sign that Libby was in full "save Irish Hills" mode.

They explained the situation, and Stone offered a ridiculous rate for J.J.'s services. To be fair, J.J. didn't have a clue what a reasonable rate for helping someone set up a salon should be. She just knew it couldn't be the amount of money Stone Stirling was throwing around. And they told her she'd have the power to decide everything.

"From décor to services offered, to staff, whatever you say goes," Stone said.

"No."

"What?" Stone's eyes were wide at that response.

"No, I said no. I'm here for a week, maybe two, and then I'm out."

"J.J.," Libby said, giving her a look that meant business.

J.J. ignored it.

"Fine, I'll double the offer," Stone said.

J.J. choked a bit and then tried to cover that up with a laugh. Doubling a ridiculous offer didn't make the idea less ridiculous. "Did you inherit a billion? Because negotiation tactics like that will have you downgraded to millionaire in no time."

"Stone, why don't you let us talk?" Libby said. "We'll catch up tomorrow, okay?"

"Okay, triple, but that's it. And you will have to buff out the Range Rover."

J.J. rolled her eyes.

Libby stood in front of her and began ushering Stone out the front door, while saying, "Triple sounds right. She's tough, but that's more like it. I'll call you with details."

Triple a ridiculous number? Sure, yeah, that was reasonable, J.J. thought and put her hands on her hips. She shook her head as the strangest visitor the house had ever entertained walked out with Libby to his janky Range Rover.

When Libby returned, she stared J.J. down.

"Do you believe that guy?" J.J. blurted. "Expecting me to work with him after all the total horse pucky he put this town through? What a joke!"

"It's not a joke, it's a great gig."

"Libby, of all people, why in the world would you be here, helping him? It was an act, right? What's the play? You just wanted to see me shoot him down, like for fun?"

"No, I want you to take the job."

"What?"

"Look, I didn't have much choice. Turns out he's holding a lot over my head."

Libby explained the situation. Stone Stirling could make or break the town, once again, by pulling his insurance coverage. "He claims he did the insurance thing to help and that he bought the grocery store to help."

"And now this salon thing? All to help? Come on!"

Libby, the invincible, plopped herself down on J.J.'s couch. "Look, I'm at fault. I should have looked deeper into the insurance company. I should have known it was too good to be true. This is on me. All the work we did to fight this guy, and he's right in the center of everything."

"I do have to admit, that grocery store *is* nice," J.J. conceded and sat down next to Libby.

"So, here's what I'm hoping," Libby said after taking a moment to regroup. "I'm hoping that he is telling the truth, that his investments are because, like he says, he wants Irish Hills to thrive. Not because he is trying to take over. He seems to want to be a part of things. That's something."

"Yeah, so why do you want me to help? He surely can hire a fancy schmancy consultant from any big city salon?"

"I want good businesses downtown. If you help, it'll be a good salon, but you'll also be able to judge better than me if he's full of it."

"Oooh, you want me to spy?"

"I guess that's it, yes. I want someone on the inside of Stone's operations here, and so I suggested a salon, and I sold you as the only person to set it up for him."

"Libby, you know I wasn't going to stay, you *know* that."

"I know, but, well…I need you. I understand you needed space; I miss Dean, it was awful what happened. It's still awful. But I need eyes on Stone Stirling, and he may have weaseled his way into town, but at least, if you're there, close by him, I'll have a heads up on whatever the heck else he's planning. If he is planning to take over or tear us down somehow...I don't know. What I do know, J.J., is that you just have to do this."

Libby was usually in the driver's seat. She was assured. She was cool. She had it all together most of the time. But J.J. could hear genuine distress in her voice, and the fear that she could lose all they'd worked for was real.

"You know, I do have some cash," J.J. pointed out all the same. "Dean's life insurance, the sale of the house. That guy can't buy me."

"He can buy just about anything, but I get it. I know. It's not the money for you. But I need you to keep your eyes on him so I can finish the reno with D.J., okay?"

Now, she's bringing D.J. into it. "What do you mean?"

"Just if I've got Stone over here, on our completed stuff, I can keep him from hovering over the stuff that is very much still completely unfinished. I can keep the pressure off D.J. a bit. He needs less pressure. I can see that."

"You're probably right on that."

"One thing is certain: I do have to have insurance, and if the project isn't done soon, I'll be begging Stone to let us stay on the policy. Let me get that other side of the street done with D.J. You keep Stone occupied and get me a good salon for this mess."

"I'm not staying. I need to see the world or whatever. I'm thinking I might wander over to the west coast." J.J. had thought she'd travel to California once Haven Beach in Florida got too hot.

"You can still do that, just after, like...get me through this summer with Stone Stirling, okay?"

J.J. readjusted her near-term plans. She thought about staying. Her house was about to be someone else's house. "Just this summer?"

"Yes. You can let me know your take, your thoughts. If Stone is on the up and up, you'll be able to see. Plus, he just backed a truck full of money up to the house and dumped it in your driveway. I know you can't be bought, but..."

"I can be rented for the summer, yeah. I do see the wisdom of that."

J.J. took Libby's hand and squeezed it.

"Okay, I'll do it. But I'm not bunking for the summer at your house. That's just too much. I gotta find a place that is less...less full of memories. You know?"

"I get it. And I want you to know you're doing me a huge favor! Stay with me, or Emma's Guest Cottage, down the beach, or the hotel across from Adrian College, whatever you need. Truly. You're doing the town a favor. Thank you."

J.J. knew even Dean would tell her to take this gig. She wouldn't even have to touch the money from the sale of the house and the nest egg of Dean's life insurance.

She could live on the windfall Stone was offering her to consult for a while. This was a no-brainer. J.J. had spent enough time worrying that checks would bounce, not to miss a financial opportunity like this.

She heard Dean in her ear: "He's shaking the money tree. Get a rake!"

On top of all that, she would be helping Libby. She'd be keeping an eye on a devious billionaire. He acted like he wanted to be a part of the town, not stomp all over it, but did a leopard change its spots?

That would be her mission, and heck, she'd spend a ton of the man's money on a salon. Her friends would at least have a place to go to get gorgeous once she left town again.

Fine. I'll do it.

J.J. may be done with Irish Hills, but it appeared Irish Hills wasn't quite done with her.

Chapter Twelve

J.J.

Nora House was almost as familiar as J.J.'s own house. But there was an element of vacation to it. It had been her escape, her fun, her view of how rich people lived, and it was the place she'd learned how to be a best friend.

Libby was the teacher on that one. And then she disappeared. They all did. The tornado scattered them just as it had scattered roofs and shingles.

J.J. had done the same. She'd moved on. She hadn't spent the time waiting for the girls to come back. She'd lived a life. And then that life was gone, and so was she. But now, here she was again. She felt like she was starting from scratch.

Even though she'd been dragged back to Irish Hills, waking up in Nora House, making it her home base at least for now, had lightened her heart.

There was no place more beautiful on earth than the view from Nora House's window onto Lake Manitou on a warm spring morning. She'd heard Aunt Emma say it many times. The woman was right.

Today, J.J. would begin setting up a salon for Irish Hills. She'd be helping Stone Stirling but really spying on him to be sure he wasn't up to something. That was her true mission and the only reason she'd agreed to Libby's plans.

She walked into the kitchen, still looking very 1980s, to start some coffee. Of course, Libby was already buzzing around.

"What time do you normally get up?"

"Oh, you know, I fall asleep at nine p.m. and then wake up at three a.m. with a hot flash. And then I start worrying about my kids, and your kids, and the girls, and the cost estimates for the plumbing in the new buildings, oh, and that I haven't finished the Dance Pavilion. So, I make coffee."

"Ha, well, the hot flash I get."

"Here." Libby handed her a brown lunch bag.

"You're kidding, right?"

"No, no I am not. You're helping me out, so I've made you lunch."

J.J. raised an eyebrow and looked inside. "Peanut butter and jelly?"

"Yes, but it's special jelly made by our Hope. It's artisanal."

"Of course. What's does artisanal actually mean for jelly, anyway?"

"No idea, but it tastes great, so go with it."

"Okay, will do. You just keep the bribes coming."

"Oh yes, I will, but I may just go straight diamonds and vintage jewels. That bag contains the extent of my cooking skills."

"Mine too, if you ask Dean. Ugh, *asked* Dean." She was doing that all the time here. She hadn't when she was off on her own, but here, it was natural.

"You know, you can say it in the present tense if you want. I'm constantly asking him questions. 'What would Dean do?' is a mantra for all my construction projects right now."

"You're nuts," J.J. said.

"Maybe. Anyway, I'd offer to drive you into town, but I do have an early meeting with an inspector."

"That's okay, I've got the old wagon from the house. And if I do decide to bolt, I'm mobile. Plus, I need to find a place. This Laverne and Shirley gig will put ten pounds on me." She rattled the lunch bag.

"Just keep an eye on Stone and set up the coolest little salon in Lenawee County. I'll shoot you over the places I know that are still for rent. It's slim pickings this late, thanks to the tourists. But I'll find something."

"Okay, I have my orders."

"And also, a bag of Bugles."

"*What?*"

"Yeah, I know you like them."

"I liked them in 1989."

"Have a good day!" Libby grabbed her messenger bag and was off to take on the world. She walked like a woman who was confident that the world would comply.

J.J. followed and headed into town, less than confident. She was actually nervous. She pulled into the spot and looked up at the last vacant space on this side of the street. She felt her heart beat a little faster and her stomach felt slightly upside down as well.

What am I nervous about?

She'd worked in a salon since high school. Her client base had been eighty-five percent of what kept Hairdo or Dye afloat for the last five years.

J.J. shook off her butterflies. She'd figure it out. She'd set up the salon, thwart any ideas Stone had about being the Austin Powers of Irish Hills, and then she'd bounce. She'd head to California for a new leg of her "See the USA" phase.

Libby had given her a key already so J.J. could check out the space and get started.

She gasped as she opened the door and took in the main room.

The space was gorgeous.
How is this space so perfect?
The ceiling was exposed, and the ductwork painted. There were also three gigantic, brand-new, modern skylights that seemed to fit in perfectly. Natural light in a salon was the holy grail.

The brick walls were vintage but also lovingly restored. J.J. knew the floor wasn't vintage but made to look like it. Wide planks, little knot holes, and gouges made it look like it was as old as the building. It was the smallest of the rental spaces on this side of the street, but somehow, that made it all the more charming. The skylights made it feel open and airy.

There was something else. Something she didn't expect.

Dean was here. His soul was in the mortar, his hands on the floor planks, selecting, eyeballing to be sure they were right. More than even in his closet at home, he was in these walls.

He'd made this space perfect, almost as if he'd known it was for her.
How could that even be?
Maybe he listened to her over the years, describing what Shelly should do at the salon to make it nicer.

"Dean Tucker, you acted like you weren't paying attention," J.J. said under her breath.

She turned and looked back at the sidewalk facing the windows. While the other retail spots had two windows flanking the front door, this had only one.

"I can grab space from the mercantile, easy enough. If you think we need two windows up front."

J.J. nearly jumped out of her skin.

Stone Stirling emerged from the back of the building, a place she'd yet to explore, too caught up appreciating the main room.

"What?"

"I can push it over. Money's not an object."

"It's not an object to you, but no."

"No, you don't want another window?"

"No, no one wants to be on display to the entire town when they're sitting there in a cape with foils. All women look like Jabba the Hut when they're in a salon cape. It's a trade secret. Trust me, one window is fine."

Stone laughed and looked at her funny.

What was up with this guy? Did he even get the reference?

She decided to explain it to him, taking it slow. "So, like, Jabba the Hut is a lumpy-looking character in *Star Wars*—"

"—I get it. I have seen *Star Wars*."

"Probably you were taken to the set when they made it or something, right?" She had no idea what the heck a billionaire did as a kid.

"Yes, my dad bought me my own spaceship."

J.J.'s eyes widened.

"Hello? I'm kidding!"

Aha, so maybe he at least got the sarcasm gene. Interesting.

"Right, sure, with billionaires flying into space every other day, it's hard to know."

"I had a normal childhood. I promise."

"Really, Mom sending you out every Tuesday afternoon to get her Virginia Slims and lottery tickets?"

"What?"

"I'm guessing your version of normal and mine are galaxies far, far away from each other."

"Maybe so," Stone conceded, "but I'm just saying I know what *Star Wars* is."

"Cool, good for you. Gold star. Let's get to work."

"Okay, let me show you around. Well, you're looking at the main space; big enough, I hope. I'll show you the offices."

Stone led the way. J.J. felt a tad underdressed any time she was in Libby's orbit, but Stone Stirling was on another level. The man's shoes probably cost what her house did. Meanwhile, she'd chosen skinny jeans and her favorite white t-shirt for today's activities. She was glad she'd also popped on her navy linen blazer. At least that was sort of businessy.

Maybe I need to raid Goldie's wardrobe for higher-end outfits? That made her think about the project at hand. She'd require a dress code here. *What will it be?*

She was momentarily lost in thought until Stone called her name.

"Uh, what?"

"This space, you've got supplies, a little office for the manager, and then there's also a break room. Is that enough?"

J.J. focused on the rooms in front of them. She walked in and out. "You said little. This is huge. There's tons of space back here."

There were more than enough places for staff to kick back, for a manager to have privacy, and a huge room for inventory and supplies.

"I assure you, one thing I do not know is how much space is required for a boutique salon."

"Your hair is perfection, don't lie. You've spent a fair amount of time in salons."

"What?"

"Yeah, I mean, white at the temples only? Come on, some high-end stylist is selectively dying it for you. Unless, unless that's a piece."

"A piece?"

"A toupee, a rug, it's really hard to tell these days."

"This is my hair! All natural."

"You can admit it if it's plugs, no shame in that game."

"Look!" Stone leaned into J.J.

She put her hand in his hair, and she tugged a bit.

"Ouch."

"Sorry, yeah, if it's implants, it's good workmanship."

"You're teasing me."

"Just a little."

And it was J.J.'s turn to laugh. Somehow, she'd goaded the

man into feeling just slightly less confident. If she was going to earn the money Stone was paying her, she needed to act like she knew what was what! She needed to level the playing field between the international man of mystery and the townie beautician.

He's a billionaire, sure, but he's also a dude who worries about his hairline. Ha!

"Okay, so we're good with space," Stone said once J.J. had stopped chuckling. "What's the first order of business, in your estimation?"

"We need to lay out the stations." J.J. walked back into the main room. "There needs to be a little waiting area here and reception space. I'd also say you want a product display. That's huge. The salon needs to align with a product line. And then, the stations take up the majority of the space."

Stone listened intently as J.J. walked the floor.

"Okay, here, that's a rough idea, and then we have maybe, hmm, let's see..." J.J. walked back and forth and then the length and width of the main space.

"What are you doing?"

"I'm visualizing." She imagined what she'd want and need for a chair, her tools, her products.

"Got it. So, what do you see?"

"Shhh. I'm thinking."

"Sorry."

She walked back and forth again and then diagonally. She decided not to dwell on the fact that she'd just shushed a captain of industry.

"Okay, I think you've got space for six stylists; any more than that, and you're looking at overcrowding. Also, it's good for business for people to think it's hard to get in, you know? Scarcity. Now, when it comes to the back rooms, if we're smart, you can turn the two areas, here and here, into a facial station and place for pedis and manis. We're not getting into waxing. That's more liability than I think you're going to want to deal with."

"What?"

"Yeah, hot wax, sensitive skin, one distracted tech away from utter carnage."

The look on Stone's face was, if J.J. had to categorize it, horrified.

"Sure, yeah, we don't want that."

"Can you imagine losing your fortune to a bad bikini wax?" J.J. cackled out loud, envisioning the headlines.

"No, I cannot. Bad investment, sure, but bad salon treatment? The other billionaires would never let me live it down."

J.J. raised her hand and conjured the headline, just for fun. "*Billionaire loses Bazillions to Bonked Brazilian*, yeah, good thing you've got me to protect you."

"So, we keep it to haircuts and highlights, manis and pedis."

"Smart man, and we'll stay away from lasers too." J.J. was making these decisions on the fly. She was seeing the salon in her mind's eye.

"Hey, I may not be a billionaire in space, but I told you I did see *Star Wars*. Lasers sound cool."

"Not light sabers, *lasers*. Another way to get rid of hair. Takes up too much space. It's not what I envision for the place."

"You're the boss."

J.J. looked at Stone and shook her head. "I'm not the boss. I'm the mastermind, the big-picture gal. I'm out of here as soon as I get you on the right foot. I've done my time behind a shampoo bowl. Managing a bunch of stylists is its own special kind of punishment."

"Sure."

"Okay, so we need to order equipment first and get the plumbing contractor in here. This isn't set up right. We need three, maybe four if it's tight, shampooing sinks right here."

"You know, I think I better write this down," Stone said, took out his phone, and started typing.

"The ordering needs to be done first, and then we need to

decide on a product line. I think we insist all the staff use it. It's critically important that we make a deal for products. I was always telling Shelly that she had a mishmash. One kind of thickening mousse, a different brand gloss. That doesn't help with consistently good results."

J.J. stopped when she realized the absurdity of having Stone Stirling take notes and follow her around like she was in charge.

"Hold on a minute, so how is this going to work, anyway? I've never consulted before. I mean, you're not my secretary or assistant." J.J. pointed to the phone Stone was hunched over, seemingly trying to keep up with her list of ideas.

"No," Stone agreed, "but I didn't get where I am today by ignoring my investments."

"Right, sure."

J.J. didn't press. The more Stone was around, the better she could keep an eye on him. And that's what she promised Libby she'd do.

Chapter Thirteen

J.J.

J.J. had two meetings. The first one was about as intimidating as meetings got.

The rep for Kedren International Products had insisted they meet in Ann Arbor, saying, "I can't possibly make it out to—where are you again? Loonawon County?"

"Lenawee." J.J. had corrected her on the phone. Loonawon was a new one. She tried not to laugh. The sales rep for Kedren International Products didn't have a sense of humor.

What she did have was the hottest, most exclusive, and honestly fantastic hair products in the world. No one in Lenawee County or anywhere in Michigan had them in their salons.

If J.J. could make a deal with the company to be the first Michigan salon to carry the line, well, that seemed like something!

She had visions of luring high-paying salon clients from Detroit.

On the day of the meeting, J.J. arrived early and was already nursing an overpriced coffee when Katie Perfoy walked in. She was rail thin, and her dark hair was so shiny it looked like it was made of glass. It was razor cut, most likely with a compass and a microscope. It was *so* straight. Her black bodycon dress looked painted on, and J.J. had to admire the bone structure on this woman. It was the polar opposite of her own short self.

J.J. stood up and offered a hand to shake. "Katie, from Kedren? Hi. I'm J.J."

"Kah-tay, my name is Kah-tay." Kah-tay did not shake hands but rather looked around and reluctantly sat down at the little two-top table J.J. had saved.

"Oh, okay, so sorry, that's lovely."

It was a lovely way to pronounce the name, J.J. admitted, but Kah-tay wrinkled her nose in J.J.'s direction. She was now holding the mispronunciation against J.J.

"I've only got ten minutes," Kah-tay declared. "I'm meeting with La Folique salon at eleven, so you'll have to make this quick."

La Folique was in Ann Arbor. It was fancy, expensive, and snooty in J.J.'s estimation.

"Oh, sure, oh, uh, can I get you an espresso or water or ah, I hear they have wonderful pastries?"

"No, honestly, less than ten minutes now."

So J.J. jumped right into her pitch. "We'd love to be the Michigan home of Kedren. I've used the products in my recent travels and just fell in love. I know that our clients will, too."

"Your clients, tell me about them."

"Well, we're situated in a resort community, and it's rapidly growing, a lot of vacationing people looking for a great salon experience. We want to offer high-quality service and skill, and of course, product, even though we're a small town."

"Hmm."

J.J. pressed on. "The idea that we'd be the only salon, that's just so incredible. We'd love to be a partner to Kedren to open the whole state up to how amazing the line is."

J.J. had no idea if she could actually pull that off, with a combination of Shelly's old client list and the handful of friends she'd bully into coming in. Still, she was swinging for the fences anyway.

"Well, you'll need to get me numbers. I need demographics. And if you have any beauty influencers, that would be something."

"Ah, influencers?"

"TikTok, Instagram?"

J.J. tried to look like she knew what Kah-tay was getting at, but she didn't, not really.

"Ha, well, I'm usually just looking at cute kitties on there, but I'll check that out to see if we have any in our area."

"Hmm."

J.J. decided to try dazzling the sales rep with her love of the Kedren product line. "I just want to say the blowout cream is amazing, and I know we'd do great things with it—and here, you can see not a flyaway on my head right now, thanks to the serum."

"Your style, though, a shag? Really?"

J.J. touched her head and suddenly was concerned that she looked like she was rocking a bouffant or something. "I'm, uh, growing out my bangs." This wasn't true. J.J. liked her style—or did until Kah-tay pointed out that it might be out of date.

"I'm running late. You've got my email."

"Sure, sure. How long would it take to get a product in if you decide to use our salon as your distribution partner?"

"It takes what it takes."

"Sure, yes, of course."

Kah-tay stood up and J.J. followed suit, quickly. In the process, she knocked the coffee she was drinking down the front of her formerly crisp white t-shirt.

"Oops, oh, ah, typical." J.J. winced as the hot liquid moved from the t-shirt to her actual skin.

Katie, uh, Kah-tay made a dismissive gesture, presumably to say goodbye, and she strode out of the coffee shop like it was a contagious disease.

J.J. sopped up the spill on her t-shirt as her mind raced

through the lists of potential clients she could lure to the salon, what their incomes might be, and if they had a social media following.

She was drawing a blank. She'd never once tried to lure anyone into her chair; and once they were there, she never worried about any of the above.

J.J. had homed in on the fact that bringing Kedren to the salon would be a huge coup. She clearly had a lot to learn about what the chic brands were after; she was determined to figure it

out.

* * *

Her next meeting was with her kid brother at his hardware store. This was more a reunion than a meeting. And it was a lot more fun than Kah-tay Katie.

And as luck would have it, Jared had a tip for her on a place to stay. A place that didn't have a million memories attached.

According to Jared, an older resident of Irish Hills was holding on to a cottage out of spite. The man refused to rent to anyone after a nasty incident last summer.

"Delbert Treach is so mad he isn't renting to anyone. Threatened a lawsuit. It was a thing. Anyway, his place is sitting there empty. He's at the retirement home, telling anyone who will listen," Jared explained.

"Treach was always mad, that I can remember."

"You got that right, Aunt J.J.," her niece Lila piped up.

J.J. looked at Lila. She had become such a beauty. She worked at the restaurant but was interested in J.J.'s new job for Stone Stirling.

"Stone's a really nice man, you know," Lila added, right on cue.

"What? He tried to bulldoze this place. Beware of wolves in sheep's clothing, girl."

"Yeah, I think you got him wrong. He was amazing on the day of the tornado. And since."

Jared squeezed Lila's shoulder. "My friend's daughter could have been blown like Dorothy to Oz that day if it wasn't for him."

J.J. was missing something, but it had been a few months. Life moves on even in a small town.

It was good to catch up with her brother and her niece. They were usually busy when the hardware store opened in the morning, but there was a little lull before lunch. It was still early, off-season. J.J. knew the store would be bustling with people getting things to open their cottages and supplies for their docks very soon.

Jared was smart and had anything needed to stock a summer place. He got almost as much gossip at his store as she used to get at the salon, and his tip on a place to stay was as good as anything Libby could find, J.J. decided.

"Give Delbert a call. Maybe you can convince him," Jared advised.

J.J. was looking to rent. If she'd been an out-of-towner or vacationer, the odds of finding something were tiny. But thanks to Jared, the hometown connections paid off.

Delbert Treach keeping his tiny cottage locked up and off the market out of spite was pure old-man logic. She loved it.

After making plans with Jared and her niece for dinner later in the week, J.J. decided to do one better than a call. She'd pay him a visit at the Silver Estates, and maybe see Emma while she was out there.

It was getting later in the day, and she knew they ate dinner early there, so she hustled out and hoped for the best.

* * *

J.J. found Delbert Treach in the TV room, watching QVC with an assemblage of other residents. It was the nicest retirement community in the county.

Emma was the most famous resident here, but J.J. also knew several other retirees in the place. Her own mother, Jackie, would probably keel over at the Tiki Bar in Winter Haven before she took up residence here.

Still, all in all, it's a lovely place to land, J.J. thought.

Delbert Treach, however, didn't see much lovely, in anything. As J.J. stood in the doorway, it quickly became evident that right now he was grumpy about *Today's Special Value.* Something about Kringle Trees being ugly.

This, according to his fellow QVC viewers in the media room, was not a shared opinion.

"They're glamorous, I'm getting one right now," said one defender.

"Me too," another added.

"Go ahead and decorate your room with pot scrubbers," Delbert scoffed. "There's a reason they're on sale."

J.J. interrupted his QVC commentary with an introduction. He said he remembered her brother and all the small-town connections were immediately touched upon.

There was a shorthand to living here their whole lives, and they both knew the language.

Luckily for J.J., Delbert Treach's patience for the television shopping channel and his fellow residents had been exhausted. She figured that was the only reason he agreed to chat about his cottage.

She knew her best play with Treach was to lay her cards on the table before dinner was served and she lost his attention to the cornbread on the menu.

"I need it for the summer," she explained. "I'll take good care of it. You know I will."

"The idiot renters last summer loved it so much they stayed

and stayed. They put in that bubbler, and then boom. I'm facing damages."

"That's terrible."

A bubbler was a machine that added oxygen to the lake water around a dock. It prevented ice from forming around the pilings and allowed a dock to stay in all winter. It saved a person time putting a dock in and out with the seasons.

But it also made the ice near it unsafe. A perfectly safe frozen lake could be made treacherous by roiling water underneath.

"You know, and I know, how dangerous that is. Of course, I wouldn't use a bubbler." J.J. was happy to play along and agree with whatever opinions Delbert wanted to espouse about any topic.

"Well, the muckity muck that rented last year didn't, and then Fred Furlong goes walking across, and then the ice breaks thanks to the bubbler, which I didn't know about. I got a call from the lawyers. Furlong got frostbite on his baby toe, which hurts like hell. And well, he's lucky he didn't drown."

"Awful."

"Right. They're still wrangling in pretrial about it. I'm going to lose my studio here and have to go down to one bedroom if I keep having to pay that lawyer. Much less if it goes to court."

"I get it. You don't want the hassle."

"Right."

"Well, you know I'm a local. No parties. I don't even have a boat, for crying out loud. I need a place to stay. Summer only."

"I got a boat. It's in the outbuilding."

Delbert was on the fence, but if he felt the need to tell her he had a boat, maybe he was thawing like the bubbled winter lake.

"I can keep an eye on things. Keep renters or kids from exploring. You know, an empty place just adds a whole different level of trouble."

"True, now that Irish Hills is the cool place. Ugh. Country music fans and hipsters. I hate 'em all."

"Right...well, I'll keep the place ship shape, and it's one less thing you need to worry about."

"Yeah, I'm going to have to sell to pay the lawyers."

"Then you should let me rent. I'll dust. Mow the lawn. Easier to sell at the end of the season if it's not mothballed."

"Clean up goose crap?"

"Yep, all of the above."

"Okay, okay. It's yours, but only because you're a local girl and because Dean gave me a good price on that roof he did."

Dean. I forgot Dean had done his roof. Of course he had.

"Delbert, just give her the keys already," said the tiny white-haired woman who had appeared behind Delbert's chair.

"Aunt Emma!"

J.J. rose and quickly found herself in a hug. The aroma of Youth Dew perfume gave J.J. the sense that she'd magically gone back in time. Emma was the same. J.J. looked closely, wondering how the woman managed to exude vitality at her age and how she had stayed so engaged in the comings and goings of this town over the decades. J.J. had thought, once, that she'd be the same, always entangled in gossip, always listening at her shampoo bowl. But somehow, over the last year, she'd disconnected from all of it.

Delbert's bubbler dispute, Stone's grocery store, and even her own son's work to renovate downtown: she'd had no interest in it or energy for it, or for anything that was related to Irish Hills. It all seemed to be a part of her life with Dean. It all connected her to things that made her sad.

But here she was with Emma and about to dive right into the deep end of Lake Manitou.

"Delbert has terrible taste," Emma was saying, "but he's meticulous about maintenance. If you can ignore that duck-patterned wallpaper border, the place is solid and perfect."

"Ducks are the decorating theme," Delbert retorted. "What would you know, Princess Quinn of the Peninsula?"

The two old timers were used to giving each other grief, that was clear.

"Give her the keys. I know they're on your ring," Emma said to Delbert. She then turned back to J.J. "He walks around here like he's going to need to unlock a car or his house even though he can't see to drive, and he's lived here for over a year."

"Be quiet, old woman."

But just as Emma had said, Delbert produced three keys from a ring that had at least a dozen others on it.

"This is to the deadbolt for the main door. That will get you in. Here's one to the boat. And this one's for the outbuilding." He put them in J.J.'s hand and then squeezed it.

"I'm only doing this for you. And for Dean. Sick of renters. I'm telling you. Sick of them."

"I promise you'll be glad you did. I'll leave it nicer than I found it."

"I know, otherwise I'd tell you to pound sand like I did everyone else."

"Well, good, it's settled," Emma stated. "Oh, and she's taking off that wallpaper. Like it or not."

"I'm just renting. I'm not—"

"Trust me, you'll rip it off with your teeth if you have to."

"Pshhh," Delbert said. "Do what you want, but ducks are good décor. It's a theme."

J.J. had no intention of decorating or renovating or even boating. She just needed a quiet place with fewer memories so she could focus on the salon, get her son sorted, and finish packing up her life in Irish Hills.

If duck wallpaper was all she had to worry about, it was hardly a worry at all.

* * *

She left the Silver Estates with the keys in hand. Her heart felt a little lighter. She'd seen Emma, and it felt good to know the mainstay of Irish Hills was as sharp as ever. Emma was like her family. She felt some guilt wash over her. She'd also abandoned Emma. Emma, who'd treated her and Dean and their boys like her own kin.

Maybe running was more selfish than I realized.

Well, onward to the Treach cottage. It would do. Maybe it would even be nice.

Her entire life in Irish Hills, but she'd never actually lived on the water. Near the water, sure; worked on the water, yes; stayed at her rich friends' places, yep, all the time. But renting a place on the lake seemed almost like a vacation.

Dean and the kids had boated on that lake all the time, but they'd never once owned a place with lake views, much less lake access or a dock.

This was a little sad since they'd lived here all their lives. But in a way, she was glad. This experience was new. Staying at Treach's had no past associations.

She'd treat it like the many places she'd stayed in over the last year. Just temporary while she figured out what was next in her life.

Duck wallpaper, Brady Bunch paneling—none of that was a deterrent. It was just a place to be until the summer ended and her check from Stone cleared.

A place to be that didn't overwhelm her with the memories of Dean. Even though he literally put up the roof that would be over her head.

Chapter Fourteen

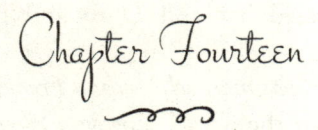

Twenty-four hours later, J.J. had moved herself into Treach's cottage. It was outdated, sure, but it was clean, it was solid, and it was clearly meticulously maintained.

Delbert Treach was a stickler, and this place showed it. There wasn't a loose screen or nail out of place. It was just out of style. And it was a little musty from being all closed up. J.J. remedied that quickly by opening a few windows. The breeze was cold, but it was fresh.

And really, the main feature wasn't the house. It was the location. The cottage was nestled in trees, hidden from the road. In fact, there were almost too many trees. But it was also on a hill, so while it was a ranch, it had a walk-out basement. The walkout was to the private beach and dock.

Delbert may not have style, but he did have sense. Nothing stood in the way of the wall of windows on the main floor or the walkout below. If you have the lake as your view, why ruin it with drapery or anything else?

After an hour of open windows and a once over with a rag and some lemon pledge, J.J. deemed it good enough to stay in.

Better than the fresh smell and view was the peace she felt in the space. It wasn't Dean's. It wasn't filled with moments at every corner. The place she needed new and fresh was her mind, and this surprisingly provided that.

Thank you, Delbert Treach!

She put clean sheets on the bed, unpacked her two bags, unloaded a few groceries, and figured she had a pretty good place to call home for now.

J.J. had a million emails and decisions to make if she was going to get the house sold and the salon open. She'd barely be here, but when she was, it would be perfect. She fell asleep to the sound of the water lapping near the dock and a bird she couldn't identify singing as the sun went down.

The next morning, J.J. got up early and was about to head to town. She'd brewed a quick pot in the ancient but serviceable Mr. Coffee machine on the counter. She'd forgotten to buy coffee filters, but as with most vacation rentals, there were countless opened packs in the cabinet. Every renter buys one and leaves it. They may have marred the lake with their bubbler, but J.J. appreciated the filter this morning.

There were a million decisions to make on the salon and on her house sale. She was about to head out the door when she glanced out the windows that made up the entire west wall. J.J. stopped. The scene pulled her away from the busy day ahead, from the errands, from the to-do list.

"Well, take a look at that," she said.

The sun crested over Lake Manitou, just beginning its ascent, really. J.J. opened the back door and found herself closer and closer to the water. She didn't mean to go to the water's edge. It pulled her gently forward.

She walked out on the dock, all the way to the end. The surface of the lake was still and like glass. It reflected the brilliant orange sun. There were a few clouds, and they, too, were glowing peach. There didn't even seem to be a ripple on the water.

J.J. had watched the sun on the beach many times since she'd run from Irish Hills. She'd seen it from Connecticut to the Gulf of Mexico. It was beautiful in all places, but today, it stopped her. It filled her up. It calmed her down. And it felt familiar and new at the same time. She used to gaze at this very water as a girl, as a teen, but not as much as a grown woman. She'd run away to do that.

The water, the wet sand of the shore, and the spring grass, still shaking off the winter frost, all told her where she was. Her feet walked confidently but carefully along the dock. A newbie she was not, and a newbie could likely get splinters on this rickety old thing.

She'd called this lake home for her entire life. Yet she'd reserved her time here for weekends and summers. Life was too busy in between those moments.

The sand was different in Michigan from the sand she'd just left in Florida. It was cold right now, but it was softer. It was more like clay here, less like sugar. But this earth felt a part of her. The hot sand and exotic salt air down south were not. Irish Hills was in her blood, no doubt.

J.J. raised the coffee mug to her lips and took a sip. As she did, her gaze shifted, attracted by a couple of swans swimming around ten feet off the dock across the glassy water toward her. They honked at her. Rude really.

"Well, hello there. I don't have anything for you this morning. But meet ya here tomorrow morning, and I promise to bring you a little snack."

They seemed to listen but then continued on.

J.J. took a breath. For a moment, she wasn't in a hurry to get something done or in a rush to block out the past. She was just there, on the dock, as the sun rose over the lake. It was a strange sensation, being there, fully there.

It was chilly, though, this spring dawn. She would remember a sweater tomorrow. And if the swans passed by, she'd have a treat for them.

J.J. turned and walked back to the house. She switched off the coffee pot, locked up Treach's place, and headed into town.

* * *

She had threatened D.J. with a haircut, so he had promised to meet her at the salon before her meetings and his construction work for Libby.

She waited for a while, but no D.J.

Finally, she called his cell. After a million rings, her son answered.

"Hey, haircut, remember?"

Her son coughed, and she heard something rustle.

"Deej?"

"Oh, sure, yeah, I forgot, on the road already."

"What?"

"Yeah, picking up some tiles for the bathroom in the, uh, west anchor building. You know Libby. She's got a tight deadline for this. So, uh, yeah, the haircut will have to wait. I'm sorry, Mom."

"It's okay, I needed to get in early anyway. Work first."

Though he said he was on the road, it sounded more like he was indoors. She heard what sounded like water running.

"Love you, Mom, thanks for understanding."

"Love you, too. But this is just a postponement. You're looking like a wooly mammoth."

"Yeah, yeah."

They ended the call, and J.J. turned her attention to the salon.

She was hard-wired to save money. J. J. had perused dozens of close-out sales and salon liquidation sales.

Her first pass, she showed Stone, and he shook his head.

"This isn't a tag sale kind of operation."

"Excuse me?"

"I want a salon that can cater to women with money."

"I want one that can cater to all women. Especially ones who live here."

"Don't they want a glamorously appointed establishment?"

"Listen, Got Rocks, you're right on the secondhand thing. I'll give you that. It's hard for me to operate in your world of not caring about price. But I don't want it so inaccessible that locals would rather drive to the haircut chain in Adrian. If it's too fancy, it's going to turn people away."

"Well, find a happy medium, maybe, but come on. I promise this place deserves zero hand-me-downs."

J.J. started again. Styling bars were highway robbery, but Stone assured her he could swing four of them, two stations each. She would start with four or five stylists, one aesthetician, and one manicurist. They'd also need a receptionist. But if she planned it correctly, they'd have space to double each if she succeeded here. Correction, if the place was a success. Growth was almost certain, thanks to Libby, Hope, Viv, and Goldie. She just had to be sure she didn't fumble the ball with the billionaire.

J.J. had spent the day ordering supplies, creating job descriptions, and working the phone for leads on good stylists to poach from the area. Suddenly, a man with a truck and a dozen chair samples arrived at the loading door.

J.J. was not expecting it and had a slight panic that she'd be on the hook for some exorbitant service fee.

"How did you do that?" she asked Stone. "They told me I would have to go to their showroom in Chicago if I wanted to try out the chairs. What's this cost?"

"This is a question you're asking me? We're the customer. They'll do what we ask."

There was a level here she just didn't understand and never would. But dang, they had the most gorgeous and comfortable salon chairs to pick from. After a day of sitting on chairs, rearranging chairs, and even spraying a little product on chairs, she'd made her decision.

The company rep was there, answering questions and even making design suggestions based on how she wanted the salon to look.

This was way better than hoping a catalog picture was accurate. She couldn't help but chide Stone for the cost of the service, though.

"I need you here, on-site, to make the decisions, not driving to Chicago," he pointed out. "I mean, even if I send you on my plane, it's time lost. We'll be spending a good chunk of money with the supplier. Time is money, so the concierge service is a savings, you see?"

"I feel like I don't get billionaire math."

By the end of the day, though, she'd zoned in on a favorite. "This one will do."

"This one? Are you sure?"

"Yes, it'll do just fine."

"It will do?"

"Yes."

"Look, this one...this one is the same look, right? But more features."

"And twice the price."

"Excuse us for a moment."

Stone wasn't as rude as you'd expect a billionaire to be, not at all, J.J. was surprised to discover. But he did expect people to excuse him, or not, on command.

Their chair concierge nodded and then pretended to have a call to take and walked out onto the sidewalk, leaving Stone to look at J.J. like she was about to be grounded.

"What?"

"I'm willing to invest in this place, make it the nicest place in the lower peninsula, and you're picking chairs that 'will do'?"

"Well, there's no need to waste money on things."

"It's not a waste to have the customers feel comfortable."

"Look, the ones I want, wildest dream chairs, are nearly three times the price of the middle-range ones, and the middle-range ones are fine."

"Come on." Stone gently took J.J. by the wrist and guided her to the worktable in the back of the salon.

She ignored the strange little jolt of electricity she felt as he made the innocent gesture.

He indicated that she sit down, put a blank piece of paper in front of her, and then found a pencil.

"Draw it like you see it. Design your dream space. I'll bring the rep back in, and we'll get exactly what you want. But do me a favor. Think big, okay?"

"What?"

"Your dream space. Dean gave the town a gorgeous canvas for all these businesses. Hope and Siena made the most of it. And you love The Mercantile next door. They all pay homage to Dean's work. Let's do the same. I'm buying, remember?"

They locked eyes. *He knows what Dean wanted more than I do?* That seemed absurd. But then J.J. thought about how much time and attention he'd paid to the historic character of each of these old buildings. She knew her husband was a builder, but it was more than that. He'd wanted these places to be beautiful, to last, to make people feel joy when they were inside these walls. Stone was right. She hadn't thought of Dean and what he'd think of this space, of how she should fill it in relation to the work he'd done.

Stone was right.

J.J. took a breath and looked down at the sketch pad in front of her. "Okay, give me a minute, I need to draw this out. Oh, and fair warning, by the time I'm done, you'll be a millionaire."

Stone laughed, nodded, and then left her with her pencil and imagination.

J.J. felt slightly off-kilter. She blamed Stone and a no-limit credit card.

Design your dream space, he'd said. *Okay. Here it goes.*

Within forty-five minutes, she had a sketch. One minute after that, Stone ordered everything on her wish list from the sales rep, who clearly saw the benefit of concierge-ing for Stone Stirling.

But her mindset had shifted. She'd been planning this like it was a chore or a replacement for the things Shelly had.

Now, this was going to be lovely and its own unique space.

Stone left her alone for most of the afternoon, and she promised that she wasn't going to try to get bargains. It was strange not to think of price, but then again, Dean had said the same to her regarding his tools and materials.

"Bargains aren't always a bargain," he'd say. "Best be honest up front, get the best quality, then you don't have me coming out to fix it later." She'd heard him say that more than once. But then he'd kept costs down by undercharging for all the work he did.

Stone was right. This space was a jewel that deserved to sparkle.

She had a late dinner planned with the Sandbar Sisters and was so lost in her new plans that she almost forgot!

* * *

She rushed over to the Hope's. For once, Hope was going to eat with them.

J.J. sat down next to Viv. She was actually hoping to show Viv some of her drawings and pictures. Viv had impeccable design taste.

Goldie was in California for a few days, making her latest deal. She'd purchased the rights to some witchy book series and was close to getting it turned into a TV series to be shot in Michigan. So, it was a table for four.

"Libby is on the way," Viv said. And J.J. handed her the sketches and catalogs.

"Just give me your opinion. Are we in the wheelhouse of classy?"

Viv laughed and started flipping through the materials.

"I ordered for everyone," Hope said. It was clear she was beat, but she also couldn't stop scanning the room to be sure her staff was living up to her standards. Of course, they were, and J.J. had never had a meal directed by Hope that wasn't perfection. But she could see Hope needed to stop and just relax. They all did. Where was the fun?

"Hope, you're tired. You need downtime, some serious rest and relaxation."

J.J. realized she hadn't been there to remind them all to slow down and have a cocktail once in a while. She was Julie McCoy, Cruise Director of their little troop...or used to be.

"I know. I know." Hope waived her off, though. She was married to the restaurant, it appeared. "There's Libby."

Libby made her way to them and sat down in the empty chair. She, too, looked a bit harried. The work of saving Irish Hills was likely never done. Though that appeared to be just the way Libby liked it. The town had given her solace in a time of need, and now she made sure the town had what it needed to thrive.

Looking at her friends, J.J. realized she'd missed her role as the fun friend. She couldn't bear to be fun in the wake of Dean's death, but maybe she'd find that again. Certainly, this lot needed a little good giggle time. She did, too, but she held back. It just didn't feel right for her to be exactly who she was before. She was different and needed to find her new way of being in this world. Still, these women were in need of a little pre-widow J.J.

"Really, I go away for a few months, and you all forget self-care and root maintenance?"

"Yeah, it's bad." Libby ran her fingers through the auburn sprinkled with gray at the temples.

J.J. had just the root touch-up she wanted to try on her. She made a mental note to add it to their list of salon supplies. Libby wasn't the only one who needed her roots done in this town. There were plenty of mid-life lovelies in Irish Hills that needed the same!

"I've had a day," Libby said.

"What's up?" Viv asked.

"Well, I just had a lot to handle. The tile guy came today, and D.J. was helping J.J. at the cottage. Totally needed, I get ya. But it was just extra today. You know how it goes." Libby smiled and took a sip of the wine that Hope had slid in front of her.

J.J. thought back to the conversation with her son. He'd said he was running an errand for Libby. But Libby said D.J. begged off of work to help her.

J.J. swallowed a sip of her wine. She felt a heat rise on her neck.

"What's he working on?" Viv asked her.

J.J.'s mind was quick. And before analyzing or thinking about the implications, her inner Mama Bear took over. "Uh, helped me get the dock in. And, uh, a leak in the kitchen sink. Thanks for parting with him today, Libby."

"No worries! He's in demand."

"Oooh, look at J.J.'s plans for the salon." Viv slid the plans over and shared them with Libby.

The conversation moved away from D.J. and to the salon chairs. They asked her about products and Stone Stirling. They also laughed about the need for facials and exfoliation.

"I used to be so dewy! It feels like an elephant's hide," Viv said as she ran her hand on her cheek, which looked lovely but could use a buffing.

J.J. smiled, enjoyed the company of her Sandbar Sisters, and even revealed that Stone Stirling, sometimes, seemed like a nice human being. They all said they'd found that to be true of late. Such a strange twist for the man who a few short years ago had planned to bulldoze the very spot they now sat.

They all enjoyed their second glasses of wine together. And J.J. did feel like she'd helped her friends take a little load off.

For her, though, it was an act. A heavy pit had settled in her stomach when she realized that D.J. had lied to her. And that, without hesitation, she'd lied too.

Chapter Fifteen

2004

"You've got the meeting with Duke Braker at one and the bid due today, too."

"I know. I know. That's why I told Branch Development that they'd get the proposal tomorrow. It can wait a day."

J.J. felt her fists curl into balls and her blood pressure go up. J.J. was not going to let this business fail. It *couldn't*.

"That's not going to get the job for you. Showing from the get-go you can't make a deadline."

"I can make a deadline."

Dean was filling his thermos with coffee. J.J. darted around him, making sure the Capri Sun was in D.J.'s lunch and the Sunny Delight was in Austin's. God forbid she mixed it up. They didn't have the same lunch period, and this was a problem so monumental that they'd likely never recover. Or at least that was what happened the last time she'd accidentally switched the lunches, and no one managed to figure out how to drink what was in their backpack for one stinking day. Pushing a straw through a pouch was Austin's Kryptonite, apparently.

But the issue this morning was pushing Dean, not a stupid straw.

"I know you can make deadlines, but they don't know that. You've never done subs for Branch Development, and they have a million options. Why in the world would they pick the guy who can't get the bid in on time?"

While J.J. rattled off the litany of reasons not getting the bid in today was bad, very bad, she wrote Austin's name on one bag and D.J.'s on the other.

She needed more bags, more baggies, and to put the wash in the dryer before they all left for the day, or else it was going to smell like mold in there. And then there were parent-teacher conferences.

Dean appeared to have read her mind about the conferences.

"I'm going to be at the school for the parent-teacher conference. I promised, and it's my turn."

With two jobs, they divided the school meetings between them, though most of the time, it felt like J.J. was the one in the chair hearing about this IEP for Austin or that pizza sale committee volunteer sign-up for the P.T.A.

She knew today she needed to do the parent thing, and he needed to get the bid in. Whatever it took.

"Look, you need that job, we need that job. Forget the teacher conference. I'll do that."

"You're booked. I saw."

J.J. had been taking every color and cut she could find to help pay down the credit card debt they'd accumulated buying equipment for the construction business.

She ran through the available options for the meeting, the clients she had booked, and Dean's business commitments. They were all spinning plates threatening to crash down at any moment.

The big picture was Dean's business; she believed that was the future for them, even if he sometimes didn't see it.

"No, listen. I've got this all covered, the boys and my bookings for today. Just get the bid done and in. That's the priority. Boys! The bus is on the way!" She yelled it, and Dean winced.

"I got 'em."

Dean and J.J. went into the hall, and miraculously, two little boys were there, backpacks at the ready.

"Your shoe's untied, Austin. And D.J., try not to use your sleeve today." J.J. handed him a little pack of tissues. He shoved them into the pocket of his jeans.

"See, we're all good," she told Dean. Turning back to the boys, she added, "Here's money for the book fair. You both need to buy a book and not a comic."

The assembled crew of little boys groaned as though she'd asked them to clean the garage or wash their faces.

"Not that Manga either, a book with words and no pictures." Despite these instructions, she was sure they'd bring comic books home anyway.

She hugged and kissed both disgruntled children, and then Dean ushered them to the door. The bus was close. She could hear it rolling toward their stop.

Dean turned and kissed her, which she received much like the boys had. He also reached around and swatted her on the backside before he headed out the door.

"For crying out loud!" J.J. said as she scooted away. There was not a scenario they'd encountered where Dean refrained from swatting her backside when it was within reach of his wingspan.

"You're sure about the teacher meeting?"

"Yes. Get the bid out. And don't forget, lean in on how you're available for all issues. On sight, SI Building is going to be the main competition and you know their foreman won't be. You're going to win on that if your bid is in the same wheelhouse price-wise."

Dean nodded to let her know he'd forgotten about that point.

Ugh. Well, at least I reminded him.

Dean and the boys were finally out the door. J.J. watched as Dean walked to his truck, and the boys lollygagged over to the bus stop. They were all three slower than J.J. would like.

Why am I always in a hurry, and no one else in this house seems to be?

She locked up the house and started running through ways to avoid canceling Tina Cavanagh's cut and color.

Tina was a good tipper and a regular. She was also a gossip with a ton of girlfriends to gossip with. J.J. needed Tina's business. She didn't want Tina to go elsewhere or, worse, complain about J.J. to all those girlfriends.

J.J. had to keep that appointment. She also couldn't ditch the parent-teacher meeting.

J.J. would figure out something. *This isn't a manned space mission, for crying out loud. I'll make it all work.*

* * *

Twelve hours later, J.J. had a round brush around Tina Cavanagh's perfect blond bob with recently refreshed blond roots. She was getting the right bend and assessing the way her hair fell.

Shelly shook the salon phone receiver at her.

"What? This is my last appointment. I can call them back."

"It's the school."

"Crap."

"I'll finish." Shelly took the blow dryer, and J.J. took the phone.

"Yeah, you need to get here," said the voice on the other end of the line. "This woman, ugh...well, it's that, or we call the cops."

"Fine, no don't do that. Where are my kids?"

"Library."

J.J. made record time from her job at Hairdo or Dye to the

school. She raced past the book sale table and the disapproving looks she knew she was getting.

She made her way to the office, and there it was, The Scene.

"Jackie. What the heck are you doing?"

"I told her that Austin failed his math assessment," the math teacher explained, "and she didn't take it well."

"Excuse me!" Jackie retorted. "I just need a smoke." She turned to J.J. "That *woman*, she's saying Austin is dumb, I won't listen to it. Just because he failed some rigged test? Please, look at Austin. He's smart as a whip. And even if he wasn't, let's say he's dumb, guess what? Who cares? He's better-looking than every kid in this school. No one that handsome needs to know fractions. I'll tell you that."

J.J. winced and hid her face behind her hand. She wanted to disappear. She'd asked Jackie for help. She'd asked her mother to do *one thing*, to cover this single meeting, and it was blowing up in her face. *What was I thinking, asking Jackie to attend the teacher's conference?* J.J. rubbed her forehead. A migraine wanted to form. She didn't have time for that.

The familiar click of a cigarette lighter put J.J. back on alert. Jackie had a Virginia Slim menthol lit up between her lips. The lines around her mouth etched deeper with the puff.

"Mom, you can't smoke in here."

"We told her that multiple times," the math teacher said.

"It's a teacher's lounge," Jackie complained, "isn't that what it's for?"

"They haven't smoked on school property in decades, Mom."

"Ma'am, coming on school grounds, smoking, and while intoxicated is dangerous for the children. And then there's the matter of destruction of property."

"What?"

"That's not what happened."

"Your mother took the binder we presented her of Austin's test scores"—the teacher paused, clearly trying to keep her composure— "and threw it across the room. It hit the computer monitor, which then fell to the ground."

"The things in there do not reflect the intelligence of my grandson, and if these cows don't know that, they're the ones who need to be tested!"

"Mother. *Enough*." J.J. grabbed the cigarette out of Jackie's mouth. She stubbed it out with her thumb and pointer finger and then dropped it into her own purse. She turned to the math teacher. "I apologize for this. If we can reschedule Austin's meeting? Maybe next week?"

"Yes, that would be best."

"Mom, come on. We need to get the boys and go."

"It's about time."

"I'm truly sorry," J.J. said again to the teacher. "I had to work and knew the meeting here was important. I just—I'm sorry."

The teacher, who all in all was a sweet woman, just young, took pity on her, it seemed. "We can do it next week. Austin will get it. I was trying to tell her that."

J.J. raised her hand. "I know, this is, she is, a lot."

J. J. loaded her boys and then her mother. Jackie wasn't drunk. She was just in a manic phase. An ill-timed one. *But then again, when were they ever well-timed?*

* * *

By the time she got her mother home and somewhat calmed down and the boys in their jammies, J.J. was beat.

Her phone rang: Dean.

"Great news, babe!"

"Yeah, less great here."

"What, are the boys okay?"

"They're fine, just Jackie fun. It's handled. What's the news?"

"Got the bid in early, thank you very much—and we got it!"

"They decided already?"

"Yep, called me a few minutes ago. You know Matty Forsythe? He's a buddy. He said they decided as soon as they saw. He called me right away."

"That's big, that's a whole neighborhood!"

"That's right, we'll be booked for a while on this one. They have forty houses, so far, in the plan."

She heard voices in the background. "Where are you?"

"Bought the crew dinner. I knew you were working, and they really put in the extra to get this, too."

"I get it, that's great. You'll need to have a good crew for this job. May as well buy them all a beer." She tried not to sound worried.

"Don't worry. They're having beer. Me? Diet Coke, and I'm going to be sure they all get home safe. Like you said. I need all of them to do this new job."

"Right." Dean was a good boss. She saw that. And he was sober. He had been. Since he promised her. He'd got the bid in. He'd taken care of his crew.

She'd taken care of everything else. But then she remembered the last few hours. She'd had a few mini disasters while Dean was having this triumph.

"You know, you were right," Dean added. "Getting it in today did make the difference."

"Wait, what? Let me get the tape recorder. I was *what*?"

"You were right, babe. Getting it in got us the work, and they loved that I was going to be available, also like you said."

"Good. Well, have fun. Congratulations. I'll see you when you get home."

"Don't wait up."

"Don't worry."

They hung up. J.J. had moved heaven and earth to be sure that nothing was in Dean's way. She knew they were a team on this, even though he got to run in for the touchdown, and she was stubbing out Virginia Slims with her fingers.

The main thing to focus on was the job. He'd gotten this big job, and they'd have a good income for the next couple of years! It was hard to see the wins sometimes when she was in the deep end of work and the kids and the bills.

But her hard-drinking, rough-edged boyfriend had turned into a responsible business owner. And a good dad. She wanted to celebrate that with him. They deserved a night out.

Maybe later, she was too tired to do anything—*oh crap, the laundry*! She'd forgotten to move it to the dryer.

Chapter Sixteen

Present Day

J.J. wanted to get her eyes on D.J. She used the haircut as her excuse. He needed one, and she was going to give him one. Period.

Even though she'd called and texted to let him know she was coming, D.J. still seemed surprised to see her. She'd arranged to do the cut early in the day at the construction trailer. He'd be hard-pressed to come up with an excuse. Plus, he'd be able to get right to work after the haircut. Her sheers and cape were packed into her tote, and her other hand balanced a Styrofoam coffee holder with two piping hot cups. J.J. didn't have an extra hand to spare, so she kicked the trailer door gently instead of knocking.

No answer. She knocked harder, and finally, she heard something, and it rocked with the footfalls of her son.

"Coming!"

The door opened, and there he was. Looking disheveled, to put it mildly.

"Mom, hey. Yeah." He was in his work jeans and a t-shirt.

She noticed a Tucker Construction polo shirt balled up on the bench near the table. She picked it up.

"It's quite a mess in here, D.J."

She didn't want to be that mom. But it was too late. She was going to be that mom. It was hard to even find a surface on which to place the coffee she brought. J.J. picked up a paper plate with a half-eaten sandwich and piled it on top of a paper towel with a pizza crust.

"This is lovely, D.J." She wanted to ground him, take away his Xbox or something, but of course, he was a grown man. Although, this was not how a grown man running a business should live or work.

"Mom, stop. Let's get this haircut done. I don't want to keep Libby waiting."

D.J. sitting was nearly as tall as a standing J.J. Her sons had gotten their father's "muckle" size. Which was apparently a Scottish term she'd learned from Dean long ago. It applied to any Tucker she'd met, man or woman. She was the odd shorty out in any Tucker gathering.

J.J. moved the pile of garbage off the table and onto the counter. There didn't seem to be a working garbage can or bag.

She headed to the trailer window. "I'm never going to get used to the man smell, never." But it was more than that. The work trailer, the one Dean had kept meticulously neat and tidy, looked more like a college dorm.

She opened a window as D.J. sat down. She slid a cup of the coffee she'd brought in front of the man-child she called her eldest.

She opened her bag, pulled out her water spray, and got going on the boy's hair.

The outdoor air helped make the trailer air breathable, and the coffee perked D.J. up a bit.

J.J. didn't want to confront her son on the lie she'd caught him in, nor the one she'd told Libby to cover up for it. She did want to see how far he'd take it.

"So, how did the tile pickup for Libby go?"

"What?"

"The tile pick up, the reason you canceled our spa day, son of mine."

"Oh, yeah, I got that messed up. Date wise. My schedule is nuts. Wound up putting out another fire instead. You know how it is. I understand Dad a lot better over the last few months working with Libby and managing Austin and the crews. The whole thing. Did you know Austin is dating a new girl? Did he tell you?"

And they moved away from the work conversation. J.J. listened to her son explain his opinions on Austin's love life and his prediction on when they'd be done with the downtown projects, and he shared some of Libby's thoughts on who she wanted to lure to downtown Irish Hills.

He was funny, insightful, and just easy to be with. She forgot the lie and chalked it up to a misunderstanding. She missed her sons. She didn't want to nag or be the fun police, so she just enjoyed the time she had with him as she cut his mop.

The little boys whom she did everything for were now men who had girlfriends, adventures, misadventures, and even shopped for clothes without her. *Imagine!*

It was still a strange thing to get used to, going from being everything for the three men in her life, to now, to being, being whatever a woman with grown children is.

Watch *Shark Tank* sometime. None of the women walk in with their invention and say, "My kids are grown, and I have this great idea now that I have time!"

No, it's all announcers declaring that this "mommy" has a great idea. Mommy is the shortest of the mothering you do, but yet somehow, it defines you to the world.

J.J. decided what her son needed was a little help. After all, she'd helped Dean build this business. She knew more about it than anyone else. It stood to reason that her young son, trying to manage it, would need a little time to get up to speed.

J.J. ran a comb through D.J.'s hair, making sure each side was even. And then she made her offer.

"Hey, looks like you could use an office assistant."

"Yeah, not in the budget."

"Well, how about your old mom and OG partner in Tucker Construction spend some time organizing for you this morning?"

"Don't you have a million-dollar salon to set up with Stone?"

"I do, yes, but I'm just waiting on some equipment to be delivered today and can't do much until it comes in. So, how about I just tidy up? File some of this, uh, paperwork." She picked up a hamburger wrapper and threw it at the wall to emphasize her point.

"I know. I know. It's a mess. I just have a lot to do. I don't have time for the paperwork."

"I'm not trying to bust your chops. I just want to help you."

"I can handle this."

"Dean Tucker Junior, this is a lot of work, this business, and you're getting my services for a morning for free. Did I say free? Your dad was a dufus, but he wasn't one to pass up an office assistant for a morning. You just go actually do what Libby needs you to do."

J.J. walked in front of her son and raised her eyes. She wanted to keep it light but also reassure him that asking for help was a sign of maturity, not youth.

"Oh, but it's not free, right?" D.J. pointed out. "I'm one hundred percent sure you made Dad pay. What about that awning you made him install on the back deck?"

"Ah, maybe so. Well, in your case, I'll just ask you to move a few boxes or something. When I move out of Treach's."

"Ah ha."

D.J. looked unsure, and despite his grown man size and beard, he looked, to her, not much different than that little boy who picked rocks from the lake shore to hand to her for safekeeping.

"Come on now, your hair is cut, you're properly caffeinated, and your old mom is here to file things. Don't look a gift horse in the mouth. Get going, and I'll be gone before noon."

"Fine. Fine. I do have to get going. Libby and I are meeting the plumbing guy today. She wants to move a bathroom. I've explained to her that it's insanely expensive, but..."

"There you go, go over to the job site and make your case with her. I still have a key. I'll lock the trailer when I'm done."

"Thanks, Mom." D.J. got up and gave her a famous Tucker Hugger. By any metric, the Tucker men were good at hugging. It was an indisputable fact.

"D.J., are you okay? This is just a little disarray, right?" She looked him in the eye. Were they bloodshot? Did he smell like a stale beer? Or was it only that the trailer was in need of a good cleaning?

"Mom, I'm not going to lie. This is hard. Not having dad here, it's a lot. But I'm getting the hang of it. Really. I promise. Austin is going to help more, too. So, yeah. I'm okay. Okay?"

"Okay." Part of her screamed it was not okay. But she didn't listen to that part. What she did was help. If she stepped back into the life she'd run from, pinch-hit for Dean, it would be okay. D.J. would be okay. She felt bad for ignoring the fact that her kids had to grieve, too. And she'd left them to it. Alone. She would fix this. That was that. She would set D.J. on the right track.

J.J. watched as D.J. left the trailer and walked across the parking lot to Libby's office. She took a deep breath. He was where he was supposed to be. He just needed help. No one could be expected to handle all Dean handled. Especially not a kid. Well, young adult, but still.

She started with the items that for sure needed the "circular file." And then moved on to invoices and work orders. She put things in the correct files. She found the box of manila file folders that she'd bought for Dean and started labeling them.

Before long, the trailer was back in some semblance of order. The way Dean used to keep it. This was going to be a big help. D.J.

would come back at the end of the day and feel calm. He'd be able to keep up a lot better without the clutter.

After a morning of mothering D.J., J.J. decided she needed to give Austin equal time.

But before she could call him, her phone buzzed.

"Hey, partner, where are you? There are a million boxes here, and your name is on 'em. Where do you need me to put them all?"

"Stone, honestly, this is clearly a matter for my secretary's personal assistant."

"Oh, my bad, I forgot their, her, number."

"His, it's a dude, male model, but your call ruined my backswing. I may as well handle it myself. But I need to take care of something first. I'll be there around two. Try to manage your empire without me until then."

Somehow, she'd fallen into an easy relationship with her archenemy, Stone Sterling. The queen of the townies and the rich out-of-town nepo baby. It was not something she would have foreseen on her bingo card. But it was kind of fun, giving him crap at every turn and getting paid for it.

She'd finish her trailer project, check in on Austin, and then get back to the salon. But she needed to hustle. The day had gotten incredibly crowded.

In an act that can only be described as heroic, J.J. opened the door to the trailer bathroom. If she held her breath, she might survive. The toilet bowl scrubber was where she'd left it, as were the cleaning products. She held her breath and sprayed Mr. Clean on every surface she could find.

She found when cleaning the bathroom of a small boy or a sasquatch-sized man, it was best to spray first, wipe with her eyes crossed so as to not see anything, and then go in again with a clearer eye. That way, anything too disgusting would be mitigated by that first pass.

These were the lessons one learned when living with all men.

That, and that it was possible to train them to put the seat down. Which she had.

J.J. returned to the trailer's restroom to something less horrifying. While cleaning, she wondered if, in the final analysis, that would go down as her greatest accomplishment.

I raised two sons who don't leave the seat up. Note to my obituary writer: that's not nothing.

Chapter Seventeen

Austin was her baby, and as such, she needed zero excuse to see him. No pretense of a haircut. His early school days were hard for him, but never because of his attitude. Austin had trouble reading, but it turned out to be tracking letters across a line that tripped him up. Once that was managed with his IEP, he thrived.

Her baby was twenty-four now. *How was that even possible?*

What Austin needed most days was Chipotle. This was the Nectar of the Gods to Austin Tucker. J.J. drove over to Adrian, grabbed Austin's favorite order, and then met him at school. He was in between classes at the community college, getting his construction management certification. Dean wanted at least one of the boys to have management classes. They had both worked for him since they were sixteen. D.J. got his training in carpentry, and Austin was always going to get the management training. But didn't. Dean's death was the push he needed to fulfill that promise to his dad. She was proud of him for doing it.

Austin met her on a bench outside the Streamer building, where they held most of the classes he needed. Austin hugged her and leaned down to peck her on the cheek. Seeing the boys made her realize with a little pang how much she'd missed them in the last few months.

She'd had no guilt, not for the entire time she was gone. She was barely handling herself then. But now, the guilt was growing. She hadn't been the person they'd needed when Dean died.

Austin assessed her Chipotle bag. "Did you ask for the double wrap?"

"You know it."

When Austin discovered he could ask for two tortillas to wrap a carnitas, he said his world was complete.

While D.J. was a carbon copy of his dad, Austin was finer built. His limbs were longer, but that said, he was still a foot taller than she was. Austin was just a little less burly than Dean and D.J. His hair was light, almost blonde, and his demeanor was quieter than his dad or his brother.

He struggled in those early school days, but he wound up on the Honor Roll in high school. J.J. was so proud. To her, the Honor Roll at Irish Hills High School was the same as getting into Harvard. She was a cliché back in the day, with a "My Son is on The Honor Roll" sticker on her back bumper. Anyone who didn't like it could pound sand.

"This is so good." He closed his eyes and enjoyed his food. He loved food as much as D.J. apparently loved beer.

"How are you doing? You seem good. The classes okay?"

"Yep."

"You know your brother tells me you're going to work with him more often."

"Yeah, really? I don't know about that."

"You know classes are important. If you think that's what you need to do, you shouldn't jump into the business too much."

"Well, I really am mostly done. Just one class now."

This wasn't the impression she'd got from D.J. He'd made it sound like Austin was nose-deep in work. And with his reading challenge, she'd let that go. Of course, Austin had to focus to get this done.

"Oh, that's good then. Dad would be very—" she stopped. She tried to drop a dad would be proud, but it caught in her throat. Her eyes welled up. *Where is this coming from? Is this ever going to get easier?*

"It's okay, mom, I know." Austin patted her on the shoulder.

"I hate being such a sap. Ugh. Okay, so you want to work more for the business, but you're not because? Explain."

"I *do* want to do more with Tucker Construction. I tried, but. Well, don't worry about it. I'll check in again with him."

Austin looked down at his food like it contained the mysteries of the universe. He also changed the subject.

"I'm dating this new girl. She's a friend of Lila's, well, the older sister of a friend of Lila's."

J.J. listened to his words, but there was clearly something else going on. She had the distinct impression that Austin was protecting D.J. by talking about his love life to her.

But it was easy to overreact. It was easy to let that Mama Bear tendency overcorrect something that her kids had to handle themselves.

She pushed her worries away and immersed herself in Austin's current conundrum of what to get this new girlfriend for her upcoming birthday.

* * *

By the afternoon, she was back at the salon.

Stone met her there.

"Our chairs! They look great. I didn't expect them here this fast."

Stone raised an eyebrow at her, and she realized he probably paid for lightning-fast delivery or something.

Well, it is his money. That said, she was going to get the dang things in position herself or die trying.

When he saw her moving the chairs from the back to the center of the salon, he was immediately scandalized.

"You're not seriously going to move large furniture by yourself?"

"I am. You can watch, or you can grab the other end."

Stone dutifully helped her move the chairs to the spots she wanted in the center of the salon space. As they lifted the last one into place, she couldn't help herself.

"Pivot. Pivot!"

"Seriously, Ross Gellar, I'm pivoting."

She laughed; *he got it!*

When Stone knew a pop culture reference, it felt totally incongruous to her. She thought of him as watching an opera or ballet or polo match, not *Friends*. But he was surprisingly down to earth.

The two of them worked all afternoon and into the evening, positioning the furniture that had been delivered that day. The mirror station placement was last.

"I think you should hold this mirror, and I should stand back to see if it's right."

J.J. had one row along the wall and a second row in the middle of the salon. She had to see it before they could nail it down, she'd decided. *Maybe both rows should be along the wall?*

Stone continued to let her take the lead and was her dutiful assistant. She'd stopped trying to make sense of that.

"Okay." Stone came over to the mirror and put his hand on the top edge above her head. He was tall enough so that she fit underneath his arm. She tried to slide away without sliding up against the man. She failed.

It was hard to ignore the fact that he smelled good. Even after a day working in the salon, he smelled good.

What was that about?

She also tried to ignore the little spark she felt when they bumped elbows or hands as they worked together day in and day out. J.J. realized that she was a hugger and a person who was used to touching people. She'd had zero of that for months as she'd traveled. She had put a wall around herself, one that wasn't natural to her.

Being in close proximity to a handsome billionaire who continued to let her buy whatever she wanted turned her head. It would anyone's. It was no more than that.

Stone Stirling had tried to bulldoze her hometown. She had to remember that. And any time she got to thinking he was a changed man, she purposefully thought back to the days, not so long ago, when she and Libby went to war to stop him.

They'd won. Plain and simple. He'd said it over and over and that he just wanted to be a part of helping Irish Hills. That was great, but still. *Keep your guard up, J.J. Tucker.* Even if he did seem sincere, he was an out-of-towner at best, some sort of corporate raider at worst.

"A little to the left."

Stone moved the mirror over.

"There! Yes! I think we have it."

"Yeah?"

"I think so, yes I do."

The space was now laid out the way she'd envisioned. There was still a lot to do, but it was finally looking like a salon. The sun had gone down, and they didn't have the natural light anymore, but the interior she'd created was sleek, stylish, and good enough for fancy out-of-towners. J.J. also thought it was cozy enough for Shelly's old faithful customers.

"Well, you've done a great job."

"I need Viv and Siena to come in and accessorize for me. Is that in your budget? I'm sure I could get a good rate for them."

"Get them in, whatever the rate is. You drive me crazy with that."

"I'm sorry, I'm never going to be able to spend money like it's from a Monopoly board. I'm not Jackie."

"Jackie?"

"My mother."

"Vodka and lottery tickets Jackie?"

"The very same, she never met a budget she could stick to."

"She sounds like my first two wives."

"Two?"

J.J. handed Stone a bottle of water from the mini fridge they'd set up in the back. She took a sip from hers. *Note to self, we'll need a bigger one once the place is filled with stylists.*

Stone had worked hard, hands-on. She had to give him that.

"I'm embarrassed to say, yes, two wives. The first wife, well, I was head over heels in love with her. She was in love with status, and then Mick Jagger, and then one of Goldie's co-stars, I think. Anyway, we had a quick divorce since, well, since it was all over the tabloids."

"Rich people, they're just like us."

"Ouch."

"Sorry, sorry, that sounds terrible. I mean, I can see what Goldie's been through."

"Wife number two, well, she was ready to have kids and wanted me to settle down and be home a lot. And I wasn't ready. That one took a lot to disentangle from. I should have made it clear that I wasn't ready for the suburban lifestyle. My fault on that second go-round."

"No kids, then?"

"One, she's in med school. I'm very proud of her. But she's closer with her mom and stepdad than she is with me."

"I see."

"Yeah, bungled things pretty good. I'm trying to work on fixing it. But probably way too late."

"Look, we do the best we can. No one's a perfect parent or spouse."

"You and Dean seemed pretty perfect."

"Well, instead of divorcing when he wasn't ready to be a family man, I stuck it out. And I mean, he was whooping it up, and I was too controlling. That was what, the early 2000s? We could have both bolted at different points, but we kept plugging, and it smoothed out, until..."

Stone didn't say anything, but he reached over and squeezed her shoulder. She felt his concern for her, and she was glad he didn't say any of the grief words. The "I'm sorry" or the "It must be so tough." None of them helped, no matter how much people meant well.

J.J. and Stone locked eyes for a second.

Why in the world does this person want to share his story with me?

Stone was one of the most elusive people out there. If you Googled him, there weren't many stories to find. He didn't play the field or date the newest TikTok model.

And yet here he was, lamenting his love life, no more successful at it than her neighbor, Stewie Richards. He'd lost one wife to their other neighbor when said neighbor got a hot tub and then divorced his second wife after she continued to get arrested for shoplifting at the Five Below in Adrian.

Billionaires, they're just like us.

And before she could stop herself, without even planning it, J.J. went out on a big limb. She just blurted it out. It seemed the most natural thing in the world. She'd gotten that comfortable with Stone Stirling.

"Hey," she began tentatively, "I don't know what you're up to, but it is the weekend. We put in a lot of time here, and if you're free tomorrow, we're going to help celebrate Keith's opening night."

Keith Brady, Libby's one true love and J.J.'s lifelong townie friend, had revived the marina restaurant. Steve's Marina Eats was now Keith's Dockside.

Hope and Keith's son, Braylon, had turned it into the coolest lakeside dining in the lower half of the state, as far as J.J. could tell.

Stone deserved to kick back, just like she did, and Keith's Dockside opening night was the perfect place to do it.

"We can worry about staffing this place bright and early Monday," J.J. finished. "What do you say?"

"Wow, yeah, that sounds about perfect. Is this...a formal thing?"

"No, it's not. I mean, I will shower. I might even wear a dress. But maybe not." She started to realize she could put in a slight effort. It was an opening and a big deal for Irish Hills.

"Wow, a regular red carpet affair for Irish Hills."

"You know it. How about this: you pick me up at my place around five tomorrow, and I promise to get you in despite everyone hating your guts."

"Still?"

"Meh, probably not, but you're so easily cocky I have to mitigate."

"Great," Stone replied with a grin, "so I'll see you tomorrow night in a possible dress. I'll dust off my tails and top hat."

J.J. envisioned the little Monopoly piece and laughed at the idea. "Can't wait."

He laughed, too.

And she scooted out of there. The word date never crossed her mind.

Chapter Eighteen

J.J. hadn't spent much time on her own beauty routine in the last few months. She, who used to keep her haircut as the perfect billboard for her services, was looking rather shaggy.

But she didn't have time to overhaul herself completely, so the next day, she gave herself a blowout and found her lightweight chambray blouse and a khaki skirt. It was about as formal as she planned to get.

J.J. slathered on a glow serum from one of the makeup samples she'd been testing. She swiped on a little mascara and some nude lip gloss. It wasn't much, but she found the older she got, the better her face looked with less. When she tried a full face of foundation and eye powders and contour, she felt like a clown.

She assessed herself in the bathroom mirror. There was one full bath at the Treach place, but it was enough. There was no full-length mirror, but if she needed a full-length look, she could use the sliding glass door. It worked in a pinch.

If not for the honking, she'd have been ready to go early.

Honking wasn't exactly the right word. It was more like a trumpet blast.

J.J. walked into the great room and looked out at the lake.

The source of the honk was immediately obvious. The large daddy swan was in her yard, honking toward the dock. She didn't want to scare the swan away. It clearly needed her help with something. She moved slowly toward the bird and saw that the male swan's white feathers were streaked with blood.

"What is it?" She moved forward, and the swan turned toward the dock. She followed as it ran as fast as an injured swan could, to the water.

J.J. walked out onto the dock, and the problem revealed itself. The mama swan hovered close to the dock and intermittently flapped her pretty white feathers. It was weird and unnatural. J.J. got as close as she could to get a better idea of what was going on. The swan's legs were moving under the surface, but she wasn't going anywhere.

"What the heck, mama?"

She looked around for the male, and he was stalking both of them at the water's edge, where it met the tree line. He gave her another honk.

"I see, I see."

Except she had no idea why he'd shown her to the female. She got closer still, and finally, the source of the issue became plain.

"Oh, you're all tangled up!"

A fishing line was tangled around one of the swan's legs and somehow also wrapped around the piling of the dock.

"Good grief, how did you get into that mess?"

She couldn't just cut the fishing line at the dock. The line was wrapped good and tight around the mama swan's leg. How would she swim that way? J.J. needed to cut her loose. She ran back into the house and rifled through a few of the kitchen drawers until she found a box cutter.

"This will do."

She was headed back out when a knock at the door interrupted her rescue mission.

"It's open. Come in, I can't talk right now. I've got a crisis to manage!" she yelled it to whoever was at her door.

"What?"

"No time!"

J.J. dashed back out to the dock, box cutter in hand, and a honking male swan seemed ready to charge her and peck her eyes out.

"Hey, back off. I'm doing you a favor."

An angry swan was no joke. His impressive wings flapped through the air, making it impossible to get too close.

Great, now big man swan is stopping me from saving his sweety. Stupid swan.

"Hey, swan, over here!"

J.J. turned around to see Stone, clapping his hands, offering a swan distraction. It worked; the male swan looked at Stone long enough for J.J. to get by. She waded straight into the frigid water of Lake Manitou, khaki skirt and adorable chambray blouse getting soaked in the process.

"Jesus, Mary, and Joseph, this is why we don't swim until Memorial Day," she said as she waded through the water toward the female swan. "Okay, okay. I'm going to have to get up close and personal here."

The male swan was somewhere behind her, pitching a fit, but she couldn't worry about that now. She needed to be fast and decisive if she wanted to save the female and get her free of the fishing line.

J.J. grabbed the female around its body and pulled the bird in tight to her own. In essence, she had the swan under her own wing. The swan didn't fight her.

"You're okay, mama, you're okay."

Behind her, the male was splashing and honking, unsure what she was doing to his mate.

"Hey, come on, here you go, over here," Stone yelled, clapping again.

"Yes! Keep daddio busy," she called back to Stone.

"Yep."

"But don't hurt him."

"I'd like to wring his neck!"

She imagined what the male swan and Stone were up to but couldn't turn to look.

"Don't kill that one while I'm saving this one."

She would need to get lower to get to where the line met the dock.

"Okay, I'm going to cut you free first and worry about the dock second. Seem like a good plan?" J.J. hoped the mama swan stayed still so she didn't slip and cut the poor thing and make it worse.

She sliced through what had to be several layers of line but held tight to the swan. If she was going to go this far, it wasn't going to be a half-baked job. She slid her free hand on the swan's two legs. They were clear. Okay, mama was free. Satisfied she'd completely untangled the swan, J.J. did her best to hurl it back into the water.

Stone's performance didn't fool the male for one more second. It flew into the lake and nearly took J.J.'s head off.

She ducked. And then she looked on as the pair swam toward the tree-lined shore.

J.J. watched closely to be sure the female was swimming correctly. She appeared to be okay, no worse for the encounter. J.J., however, was suddenly shivering. She was standing in cold water, soaked from head to toe. She looked at her fingers, still wrapped tight around the box cutter. They were blue.

"Come on, get out of that water. You're shaking!" Stone offered her a hand and hoisted her up on the dock. "I've never seen anything like that."

"Like what?"

"You grabbed that bird, and just, I don't know. Took charge. It was impressive. I mean, how in the world did you know what to do?"

"She was trapped. I had to get her out. Not too much of a pppp-uzzle there."

Stone pulled her to him; he was warm, thank goodness. *Warm.*

"You must get inside, Sheena, Lord of the Lake."

"I ddd-do."

A short time later, after a hot shower, she'd thawed out. Her hair wasn't quite as cute as she'd done it the first time, but it was dry. Now she had no choice but to wear a stupid dress. She found her black jersey dress from Amazon and a short jean jacket. This would have to do for the dockside opening. She reapplied the makeup, but this time, did add a little color to her cheeks.

"Two getting readies in one night is two too many," she said to her own reflection as she grabbed her purse.

J.J. found Stone just standing at the water's edge, waiting for her.

"What?"

"Look here."

She looked down, and there it was, a little nest of cygnets. The mama swan was now sitting with her babies, keeping them warm. The male wasn't in the vicinity at the moment.

"Where is the male, do you think, off getting food?" Stone asked J.J., like she was a swan expert. She was not.

"If they're lucky. But he was injured. His feathers were bloody. Maybe it happened when he was trying to get her free?"

"Too bad, we could maybe get him help, too."

She thought of the male swan; no way he'd let her get near enough to take him to a vet. She supposed she could call the Michigan DNR.

"It's likely he's out there and well...you know." J.J. felt sad thinking of it.

"Well, they're lucky, lucky you were here and knew what to do."

"Thanks, yeah, I'm glad at least the mama is here with the babies."

They just stood there for a while and watched the fluffy little babies with the mama.

J.J. felt like she needed to find food, too. She'd help the mama feed the babies.

Because, somehow, she knew the dad was gone for good. He'd figured out how to get Mama free, and she knew he'd died doing it.

Chapter Nineteen

Stone

Stone had arrived early to J.J.'s the evening of the "Great Swan Liberation Caper" because he was excited to see her. There, he'd admitted it to himself. J.J. Tucker was becoming his favorite part of the day.

When he arrived, he did not expect to find her running around with a box cutter. But there it was. There were a lot of unexpected things happening to him these days.

There was something different about J.J. Tucker. She didn't care about status or money. A lot of her people were the same. But while her circle of friends did have those things, money or prestige in their fields, they'd all decided that Irish Hills was where they wanted to be. They'd all come around to the life that J.J. Tucker had all along.

He wondered about how she'd felt, leaving it all behind when she ran last year. Working with her was endlessly interesting to him. And maybe someday she'd trust him enough to open up more about her grief.

It was easy to see why her husband had died saving her.

In the swirl of the storm, Stone had seen it unfold.

He knew that the tornado had changed his life just as it had changed J.J.'s life.

He was moved that day and in the days after.

There was something about being on the ground, in it, and ultimately with the people of this tight-knit little place that shifted his view of what mattered in the world.

It's not that he hadn't helped other places, or things, or companies, or even charities.

Stone Stirling had invested his money into businesses he felt were profitable in his younger days. Now, with such wild success, he was on the hunt for ways to give it away. That was part of the shift: how could he do good with this money that now multiplied without him even doing anything.

Over the years, he'd built things—or thought he had. But honestly, he saw now that what he'd done was fund the work of others. And not even that. He'd funded companies that funded companies that built things. If Dean Tucker was hands-on, Stone Stirling was hands-off, on-high, too far away to say he built anything.

At fifty-five, he'd experienced so much. Been so many places. But this place was different. Just like J.J. was different.

The day of the tornado, he'd heard the wail of the siren and then the roar, like a freight train. There was no mistaking when a tornado was coming.

He'd been in California during a huge earthquake and, of course, hundreds of small ones. He'd been in Miami during Hurricane Andrew.

But this was different from those events. There was no warning, really. The siren was almost too late. While meteorologists can track the exact path of a hurricane, days before landfall, the tornado explodes in the sky. Two opposing forces swirl and create something fearsome but also random.

When Stone saw it in the distance, it weaved and leaped and jerked. His first instinct was to go high, like for a hurricane. You needed to get away from the water in a hurricane. But here it was different. You need to get down. You need to hope it skips over you.

He'd been in his SUV coming from the airport when he heard the sirens. Even last year, he was changing. He'd started to eschew having a driver and an assistant.

Normally, he would be in the back seat, on the phone. It was his habit to not look at the landscape. It was his time to catch up on work while he was in transit. But he'd realized how many vistas he'd missed by doing that. Stone was trying not to miss the view when the view turned dark that day. And there was no driving through it. He'd need to get out of his SUV and take cover. He only had seconds to decide.

He pulled up to Barton's and got out of the SUV. That's when he saw the girl. Maybe she was ten or twelve? The kid was alone and paralyzed with indecision outside in the grocery parking lot, like he was. Her long red hair was whipping around, and she stood and circled in the same place. She needed to run but didn't.

Seeing her snapped Stone out of it. "Hey! Come on!" He grabbed the girl's hand.

"I was trying to get to the store, and my dad is..."

"No time." And that was it. There was no more time. Getting inside the grocery store or anywhere else was impossible. The twister was there. He took the girl and dragged her to the far side of his SUV.

"Crawl under there!" He didn't know if that was even the right thing to do, but it was better than getting hit by a flying limb. He hunched down, back to the wind, and covered his head. The girl was half under the car. The rattle and roar surrounded them. He peered through his elbow to try to see what was happening.

Stone saw a man in work boots and jeans running toward the

town. *Who in the world would run toward it?* Stone ventured another glimpse down Main Street.

It was Dean Tucker, and he was waiving people into the beauty parlor. He recognized J.J. in the distance. But he couldn't hear anything but the wind.

Stone had to hunch down again as sand hit his eyes. "Stay down, it's here!" he called to the girl. And that was all he actually saw. He heard the crashing. The snapping of lumber. It was a cacophony of destruction all around him.

For a terrifying moment, there was an absence of sound. Something seemed to suck the air away. There was an unnatural silence. And then the pressure released. It made his ears pop like a rapid descent in an airplane.

The monstrous thing was gone. He saw its dark talons on the horizon. But it was moving away.

"Okay, come on out."

The girl crawled out. He took her hand. He looked her up and down. She was stunned, clearly, like anyone who saw that thing. But she seemed unharmed.

"What store were you going to?"

"What?"

"Where's the store your dad's at? Can I help you get there?"

She looked past him, and her eyes were wide. He turned to see what she was looking at, and it was Barton's. Or it used to be Barton's. The grocery store was gone. What was left was twisted. Mangled. But there wasn't much left.

"Is that the store?"

"Uh, no, thank God, no. My dad was in the hardware store. I wanted to go to The Mercantile." She pointed to the hardware store down the street.

"I don't think you should be walking by yourself, there's lines down, there's debris."

"Yeah, right. I mean—what in the actual?"

This was his thought as well. Leave it to the kids to find the right phrase. *What in the actual?*

"Come on, I'll drive you over there." Slowly, he maneuvered his SUV toward the hardware store. They didn't speak. It was all they could do to process what they were seeing. He helped her to the hardware store and even walked in with her, just to be sure.

There was so much havoc and chaos. Completing this small thing helped him make sense of it. Just make sure this kid is safe. As they walked in, Jared Pawlak—he knew Jared was J.J.'s brother—came running out.

"Daryl, she's here! Oh, man, we were freaking out."

Daryl was apparently the girl's dad. The man looked like he'd been through hell and back. "Brittany Nicole!" he exclaimed. "You scared the crap out of me. Where the heck—?"

"I got caught in the street. This man helped me."

Stone nodded, and Daryl put a hand on his shoulder.

"Thanks, man, thanks."

"Sure, of course, it happened fast, you know?"

Stone watched the relieved dad hug his daughter. He felt his own relief. This was a happy ending.

He also felt a lot of regret. He had a daughter too. *Where is she right now? Does she know that I'd be there for her in a storm? Or for anything?*

She was grown, not a little girl anymore. He'd let her mother be the main parent. He was the afterthought, at best.

That was no one's fault but his own. He knew that.

All this stuff came up, right there in the hardware store, kicked up like the wind of the tornado. He stood there and evaluated his life and his relationships.

Watching the father and daughter and, earlier, seeing Dean Tucker walk through a tornado to get to his wife, those things opened Stone's eyes. There were connections between people here that he did not have in his life.

Once his eyes were open, watching the town come together after the tragedy of the tornado changed him to his core.

First, it was the chainsaws. Everyone with one got it out and started cutting limbs out of the way of roads and driveways.

There was the frantic effort to save Ned Barton, though it was for naught; everyone in town helped the fire rescue do what they could.

After the rescue turned into recovery, Stone watched the love and care each member of Irish Hills gave to one another.

Even people he knew to be at odds with each other, not even friends, seemed to be family to each other at that moment.

He didn't have a chainsaw. But he had other things.

The grocery store. The insurance company. Even water. He could get water here for everyone helping in the cleanup. So, he did that. This time, he didn't have a man or an assistant do it. He did it himself.

He made calls. Rented trucks. He loaded and unloaded. He drove things back and forth and even got a thank-you hug or two.

This was new. This getting your hands in there and helping other people. He'd never once seen things like this in action. He'd never once had "boots on the ground," as they say. His life had insulated him from it. And in the end, that had made his life less. He saw that now.

Stone had a lot of ground to cover, but he understood that he needed real connections. He needed real community.

He wanted his daughter to know he was there for her. He didn't want to just underwrite or fund or donate to something that would donate to something else. None of that was a real connection. *Connection.* That was what he'd been missing.

He wanted to be like the guy who owned the hardware store. He wanted to be the dad hugging his little girl. He wanted to be the man who ran to help his wife no matter what the obstacle.

This was the life he had missed.

He didn't know how to get it exactly. But it seemed to start with just showing up. The people of Irish Hills showed up for each other.

He also wasn't an idiot.

The woman whom everyone in town leaned on was Libby Quinn, and before her, Emma Ford. Instead of doing the opposite of whatever they did, he was going to follow their lead. He was going to stop getting in their way and start getting on their page.

The tornado was a turning point for him.

Sure, he got punched in the face by Libby Quinn at the jump, but that was a badge of honor.

And now, he'd just helped J.J. Tucker liberate a mama swan from a fishing line like it was the most natural thing in the world.

I've got boots on the ground. Well, in this case, the lake.

Chapter Twenty

J.J.

J.J., in her revised outfit, stood with Stone watching the mama swan. Stone was wearing jeans, a casual polo shirt, and boat shoes. This was a much more dressed down Stone Stirling than she'd ever seen, even the days they worked in the salon.

When he tore his eyes away from the nest of cygnets, he said, "Wow."

"What? Do I have lipstick on my teeth or...?"

She did not feel like her dress was "wow." But maybe it was the jean jacket, a Goldie castoff, that upped her look?

"No, just, you look so pretty."

He had to be joking. Pretty? He was used to supermodels and whatnot.

"Great, you're drunk. Give me the keys."

"You need to learn to take a compliment. In English, the customary response would be, thank you."

"Ha, ha. Let's go." She laughed.

Stone didn't.

Oh, he wasn't joking about the pretty thing. Well, what do you know about that? I look pretty. And I like hearing it from Stone Stirling. Will wonders never cease?

"We better get going. My little swan escapade has us a little late."

Stone offered her his arm.

"Come on, it isn't prom."

"I was raised with manners, so you know, this is manners."

"Your nanny teach you that?"

"Yes, bingo, now let me assist you into the car so I can close the door and not hear you for ten seconds as I come around to the driver's seat."

She slugged his arm and then took it as they walked to his SUV. She'd opted for sandals with a tiny heel, but a heel could mean disaster. If a man offers to help you avoid disaster, don't be an idiot. Take the help.

She got in the car and made a zip across her lip.

"My gift to you, ten seconds," she staged-whispered.

He laughed and closed the door to her side.

J.J. felt pleased. *This is going to be a fun night with old friends. And one new one. One very unexpected new friend.*

* * *

Keith's Dockside was exactly what Irish Hills had been missing. A place where you could dock your boat, get out, get a meal, get a beer, and get together right on the water.

J.J. thought the girls might tease her for letting Stone Stirling drive her over, until she remembered that it was Libby who had insisted she keep an eye on the billionaire. So, she was simply working her covert mission, right? Not dating Stone Stirling.

She also knew she wasn't on a date because she was over fifty, was completely comfortable with Stone, and not trying to impress anyone.

J.J. imagined actually dating in her fifties would be a nightmare trapped in another nightmare. She had no interest in that whatsoever.

Thanks to the last few weeks working shoulder to shoulder with Stone, she felt at ease in his company. They spoke the same language about a lot of things, and when they didn't, they found something to laugh about instead.

They slid into Keith's Dockside without fanfare. The party was in full swing already.

"Can I get you a beer? Looks like it might be a bit of a wait."

J.J. looked over, and the two bartenders were moving fast. She recognized one as Keith's son, Cole. The other was new. "Yes, thanks. No hurry. I'm going to find the girls."

Stone nodded and moved through the crowd to complete his not-so-covert mission.

Soon, Libby, Goldie, and Viv had reeled her into their corner of Keith's. Libby was in her classic white t-shirt and linen palazzo pants. Goldie had a fabulous kaftan on, no doubt courtesy of Viv's line, and Viv wore a mango tunic with white jeans.

They're all so effortlessly gorgeous. Though, they all need a haircut. She'd need to get that salon open pronto!

The restaurant was full, but not so loud they couldn't talk.

"Wow, Libby, Keith did a great job," J.J. enthused. "I thought this would be like Steve's Marina restaurant part two, but this place overshot that vibe by a mile."

"It's not stuffy though, is it?" Libby asked.

"Not in the slightest, I just mean it's cool. Very cool."

"Keith, Hope, and Braylon are a force." Keith's son had helped Hope to launch her restaurant.

"Yeah, so is Braylon going to be mainly here now?"

"That's the plan. He's running this place, so Hope is in the market for a sous chef," Libby explained. Hope was at her restaurant and promised to be by Keith's later if she could get away.

"I recommend she hire a twenty-something woman with a

good work ethic, tolerance for big lugs, and openness to a potentially meddling mother-in-law."

"Yeah, for Austin or D.J.?"

"D.J. for now. I guess Austin isn't ready to get married and has a girlfriend, but for D.J., it's past time, in my opinion."

"He's got the business keeping him busy," Viv said.

J.J. noticed that Libby looked away from them and then stared down into her drink.

"How's the salon coming?" Libby asked, changing the subject. "Anything I need to know about?"

"I hate to say this, but no. Stone suspiciously continues to support my ideas on the salon. And even had a few good ones of his own."

"So, he's not trying to torpedo it or bring in some competition or goodness knows what? He's done everything he can think of to be a thorn in our sides."

J.J. was irritated to hear Libby complain about Stone. "No, if he is, he's hiding it well. I hate to say it. I like the man."

"Whoa, that's it, now we know, these drinks are way too strong," Viv joked.

"Right," Libby laughed.

"I haven't even had one," J.J. pointed out, "so there. But you two were the ones who'd said he was on the up and up. You were right. I was once in a row, so far, wrong."

Libby put a hand to her forehead as though she was going to faint.

"Alright, alright."

Stone arrived with the drinks. "Are you okay, Libby?"

"I don't know. J.J. just said she was wrong about something. I'm not sure if I'll actually recover."

J.J. took the beer Stone offered and then sucked down a long cool sip.

"Her instincts are good," Stone said. "She spent the morning the other day doing books for D.J. and the afternoon haggling with a hair color distribution company. I can't believe she was wrong in any capacity."

"That's a smart man," Viv said, clinking her glass with Stone.

"D.J.'s books? Why are you doing D.J.'s books?" Libby asked, and there was an edge to her voice.

"I used to help with Dean's. Same thing."

"Dean had an accountant, a CPA firm, that I worked with extensively," Libby replied. "The key to keeping Dean's schedule and budget was keeping the numbers on point."

J.J. didn't like Libby's tone. "How do you know what the key to Dean Tucker's business was?" She smiled when she said it, but she knew there was now a matching tone to her voice.

"He went through costs line by line on all our projects. It was meticulous."

Viv and Stone stood back as the two women squared off. J.J. didn't like the way this was going.

"I did Dean's books, secretarial work, scheduling, bid prep, and just about everything else in his early days. I know full well that when you're starting out, you need a Gal Friday."

"D.J. had full access to my assistant and to—" Libby stopped then, seeming to swallow whatever next point she wanted to make.

"Look," J.J. said. "I'm going to help my son just like I helped Dean, and I did help Dean, even if you were out in the world living your life when we were here building ours." J.J. was probably too curt, too hurt, to soften her voice when she said it. But she wasn't going to feel bad for helping D.J. He needed support, and she was now here to give it.

"No, sure, yeah, that's right. I'm sorry. I think of him as at Dean's level, and he just started out."

"Right. It's going to take some time."

"Sure, yes, of course." Libby put an arm around her, and they squeezed each other. They were BFFs. Their relationship wasn't so delicate or precious that it couldn't withstand a little tiff.

If that's what this even was.

The tension between them further dissipated when Keith made his way to their part of the booming party.

"Keith, this is amazing," J.J. told him. "You brought it back to life and then some."

"Thank you, high praise! Look at this. Two townies make good."

Keith was from Irish Hills, like J.J. They were the only two who stayed year-round. They both used to count down the winter days until their friends of summer would return.

J.J. felt so happy for him. She'd been there when his wife got sick. When he'd watched her fade away. He deserved this second act. So did Libby.

For a moment, J.J. was overwhelmed with love for Keith. He understood what it was like to be left alone the way she had been. Keith had moved forward. Maybe she could, too, someday. She hugged Keith, and he hugged her back.

"You're lookin' good, kid. Glad to see you out here having a little fun in Irish Hills. It's not the same without you."

"Shh, they think they're in charge," J.J. whispered in his ear.

He laughed.

* * *

It was a fun night, and Stone didn't hover around. He seemed to have some friendships now with people in Irish Hills.

Hmm. I went away for nine months, and things sure did change. The former pariah has lake buddies.

Later, when things quieted down, J.J. was ready to go. She'd had fun, laughs even, but her days of staying up all night were long behind her. Fifty was like being a toddler; you needed naps and a bedtime to properly function.

She remembered Stone had driven here, so it was time to find him or call a cab. Since cab service was sparse in Irish Hills, she hoped he was ready to go, too.

J.J. was rounding a corner when she heard her name come out of Libby's mouth. She stopped in her tracks and hung back in the shadow of the hallway.

"J.J. is blind to it. I think she's hurting D.J. by coming to the rescue."

It was Viv who spoke next. "It's really hard not to help someone who's struggling with addiction, doubly hard when it's our own kids."

"I know, I know, I understand that. But D.J. is lying to her. And to everybody. I paid an accountant; he told me the accountant was doing the work. And you heard her."

"Well, maybe the accountant did some work, and she did some work. Both could be true."

"Yes, you're right. And it's my fault, too. I had her come back because I wanted her to help him. But I guess I was hoping it would be a tough love kind of thing. Dean would have handled this differently, I think. She's helping, but what worries me is that it's enabling, and D.J. is getting worse. The work is getting worse."

"It's not our business, their relationship."

"But D.J.'s business *is* my business. If we miss deadlines on the project, if we fail, there are ramifications."

Someone in the bar laughed, and others joined in. Libby and Viv moved away. They hadn't seen J.J. They didn't know she'd heard their conversation.

Her initial instinct was to charge in to defend her son. But this was Libby and Viv. In that moment, if she butted in, she'd be fighting with Libby. She very well wanted to say something she knew she would regret.

D.J. needed her help, and she was giving it. He liked his beer. That was it. Libby didn't know a thing about it. Her kids were different from J.J.'s. To Libby, soccer was a contact sport.

Her boys were tough. They were brawny men with big appetites. The disparity between the privilege that Libby's kids enjoyed and what her kids did not as they grew up seemed like a canyon.

That canyon of difference stopped her from going in and popping off to Libby. She was going to give Libby grace. Libby was worried about D.J.—that, at least, was a good instinct.

Still, it hurt to her core, hearing their unfiltered conversation about her and her son. She wished she hadn't.

And, big surprise, Libby's method of parenting and J.J.'s were different. Of course, they were! Libby had nannies for her kids. A housekeeper. She was raised that way, too.

J.J. and Dean were hands-on. They were present. Her kids were used to having help from her...and then Dean goes off and dies!

J.J. had left D.J. to fend for himself for nearly a year, and he'd just lost his dad. This was, in part, her fault. She did have to fix it. Of course D.J. was off-kilter! And, of course, now she was there to set it right.

Libby didn't understand that. D.J. was fine, and whatever help he needed was normal.

She was there to lend her support, just like she'd done with Dean when he started out in business. No more, no less.

J.J. felt sick. She just wanted to get out of there. Her mouth would likely make this worse if she said what she wanted to Libby.

And she usually did.

J.J. found Keith one more time. She hugged him congrats and did the same with Viv. It was a huge effort, suppressing her temper, but now she was tired. She needed to go. The party, for her, was over.

Stone found her as she searched the room for him. He put a gentle hand on her elbow. "You disappeared."

"You ready to go?"

"I can be anytime. Are you okay?"

"Yes, why?"

"Your face is a little flushed. You look sort of panicked."

"I'm fine, just done. Yeah, let's go. I already said my goodbyes."

"Gotcha."

Stone helped her navigate the room, with a hand on the small of her back now. She wondered if she would have thought more about that if her mind wasn't reeling as it replayed Libby and Viv's conversation.

As it was, she was grateful for the help to get out of there. She wasn't overprotective. She was the right amount of protective. And she wouldn't even be here if not for Libby tricking her into coming back.

Maybe that was the mistake. This was all just fine while she was out traveling.

Or was it?

J.J. felt sick to her stomach, her head hurt, and she felt bone tired.

She sank into the seat of Stone's Range Rover.

"Kiddo, you look like a truck hit you in there."

"I think it did. I really think it did."

"You can tell me, or we can just drive. Whatever you need."

"I don't want to talk about it."

And then J.J. recounted every syllable she'd overheard to her new friend Stone.

Chapter Twenty-One

In the days following Keith's opening night, J.J. put her head down and focused on two things: her son and the salon.

She begged off when Libby asked for lunch. She didn't have time to gab with the girls. She'd promised Libby she'd get the salon off the ground, and she was doing that.

She was also watching D.J.'s back. She checked his calendar, reminded him about appointments, and slyly, she thought, ensured he succeeded. He was fine.

By early June, after a mad dash of work and hiring and decisions made, the salon was ready for a soft open. She'd cooled off from her irritation with Libby, and the soft launch was the perfect opportunity to reconnect. J.J. could play nice again. She knew her friend meant well. She knew that. It was just hard to take when it felt like someone was attacking your kid.

The salon wasn't public yet, but having Libby, Goldie, Viv, Hope, Siena, and even Emma in to get their hair done and use all the services they had to offer would be a good trial run.

They could test their systems; they could show off their work. It was a good way to start, especially for the new employees they'd hired. They also had their new employees pick two or three friends and family to come in, too. They'd be busy, but it would be fun and low pressure.

Well, low pressure for everyone but me.

What they didn't have yet was a name.

"I'm telling you—this should be *your* place."

Stone wanted J.J. to be the permanent manager. She tried to imagine it. Every inch of this place was first Dean's; now she'd made it hers. She'd decided everything from where the chairs sat to the name.

But something held her back. Stone wanted to hand her this place on a silver platter. She should take it and run with it. She'd never dreamed of opening her own place. She never thought it was even in the realm of possibility. Maybe that was it. Maybe her friends all had big city dreams, and hers were small. And that was fine. Her dream turned out to be Dean and their life together. She'd had her dream. So she kept her hands down and did not take what was on that silver platter.

The hour before they opened the doors, for the first time, Stone pushed her again. "I'd be a silent partner. You already run this place."

"No. I'm not in the market to run anything. The contract we have does not include me doing this permanently. Remember, I'm out after we launch. However, I do have issues with those managers we interviewed. I think one is—"

"—Ha, see, they're not you; that's the issue. I think you're selling yourself short. You could have salons all over the country."

The man thought in terms of world domination. She thought in terms of checking to be sure the new shampoo girl knew to empty out the lint trap after they dried a load of towels.

"Ha, I could be a chain!"

"Wait, isn't that from *Steel Magnolias*?"

"Something like that. You're good, Stone, I'll give you that. Now get that box up there, could you?"

Stone lifted a box of their custom product onto the table.

"Okay, moment of truth."

Stone watched as she opened bottles. She'd formulated a few products that she liked on Stone's dime with one of the millions of companies he was connected to.

After they'd got the runaround from Kedren, Stone let her in on the secret. They could pretty much find a dupe and label it any way they wanted.

"They can only get the stuff here, with your staff; that's pretty scarce, and scarce is good business."

"You should know."

She pulled the shampoo bottle out of the box, and her jaw dropped open. "It looks so good!!" She turned the bottle around in her hand. She'd selected the logo to match the name of the salon.

Stone had wanted to call it J.J.'s, but she refused. After a few brainstorming sessions and a call to Shelly, they'd come up with a name.

"The Do."

It was a nod to Do or Die Job, and somehow, it also sounded modern. The Do logo looked great on the product line, too. The Do in Irish Hills.

They heard voices in the salon. It was time.

"Well, I know you don't want me to give this place to you. But if you did, I would." Stone was serious, and when he looked at her, she saw his admiration and respect. She now felt the same about him. He'd become a part of Irish Hills in a way she never would have believed back in the days when he was swooping in via limo with a team of lawyers.

She'd seen not a single handler or lawyer or assistant the entire time they'd worked together.

"I appreciate that. And it's the thought that counts."

The sweet moment turned into a frenzy of people coming in to get gorgeous and loving The Do. J.J. swam like a shark for hours among the hair stations, the shampoo bowl, and the mani/pedi room.

"I look like Helen Mirren!" Emma was admiring the style Vickie had shaped for her.

Emma had mostly rocked a modern bouffant hair shape since J.J. had known her. If it was good enough for Betty White, Emma said, it was good enough for her.

But on soft open day, Emma said she wanted to be a walking billboard, a real live model, for The Do. Vickie Linyard did her hair. And Emma wasn't wrong. The bouffant was now a stylish bob with wispy bangs. Vickie had used a toner that had turned Emma's sometimes yellowing white to icy brilliance.

"Better!" Goldie said as the two women admired their new hairdos.

Goldie was a high-pressure customer, too. Movie star hair was another animal. It had to be *vava-voom* at a moment's notice. Mason Bennett was the man for that job. He was young and talented. He'd only recently finished school but had a passion for going to the latest hair shows and learning the newest techniques. J.J. didn't think Mason would be long for Irish Hills, but if, while he was here, he could style an internationally famous Oscar-winning movie star? Well, there were worse ways to build a resume.

"This, this really works, I never part it that way." J.J. eavesdropped as Goldie and Mason discussed the finer points of the placement of Goldie's part. Emma agreed it was a radical change!

Meanwhile, Libby had her roots done, Viv got a facial, and Hope a pedi.

It had all gone without a hitch. And everyone was treating J.J. like she'd just won an Oscar herself. She kept pushing the compliments aside. *It's a salon. A nice one, sure, but it wasn't curing cancer, for crying out loud!*

Libby caught up with J.J. as she was overseeing her niece Lila on the credit card reader and scheduling software.

"You're going to pretend to charge, run credit cards but

refund. We just want to be sure it all works. Just do that for the Sandbar Sisters. They're aware we're going to use them as guinea pigs."

"Got it."

Lila had decided to jump from Hope's restaurant to the duties here at the salon. J.J. hadn't wanted to raid her friends' businesses to staff this one, but Lila was family, after all. Also, the pace at Hope's had picked up so much Lila said it was feeling like real work: "Here, I can sit sometimes." That said, Hope didn't seem to have a problem finding young culinary students and foodies who wanted to work at her oh-so-trendy bistro.

Libby waited until J.J. finished coaching Lila.

"You did it," Libby said. "This place is stunning. So gorgeous."

"Thank you. Is it too much?"

"No, you had the budget of a small city, thanks to Stone, no way too much."

"No, I mean, well, it's so posh."

"I think Irish Hills has got enough posh summer clientele these days to warrant a little putting on the dog, as Emma would say."

"True."

"I wanted to check in. You seem, well, distant. Are we okay?"

"Oh, me, yes, I just was, you know, doing all this." J.J. waved her arm around to the now-completed salon.

"Gotcha, so, what's your take?"

"On?"

"Stone. Is he okay? He never tried to undermine or undercut or, I don't know, bring in an out-of-town investor we don't trust?"

J.J. thought about Stone, and her changed feelings for him. She wanted to give Libby her thoughtful and measured opinion of the man. But the words in her head were all superlatives. She realized that thinking of Stone made her happy. But she stopped short of sharing that.

"You know I wanted to hate him; I did hate him. And I've

done exactly what I thought needed to be done here with zero undermining. If anything, he pushed me to make it nicer, not cheaper. Not sure how you stay a billionaire spending like this, but I guess this is still small potatoes."

"It seems like you're not giving me the full story. You didn't catch him trying to sabotage this in any way?"

"Ha, no. Not at all. He just wanted this to be another great place in Irish Hills. The guy learned to use an Allen wrench, for crying out loud. He's come a long way."

"Thank you. I'm so glad you got this going and kept an eye on him. I've had my own plates spinning. I wonder, in the next few days if we could talk, just us. For coffee."

Something made J.J. hesitate. She didn't want advice from Libby on how to be a mom. The conversation she'd heard between Libby and Viv still stung when she thought of it. She'd kept her mouth shut and suppressed her desire to go to battle for her kids. The last person in the world she wanted to battle was Libby.

That said, she wasn't sure if she could trust herself to get coffee with Libby. And put things on the table.

She'd get over it. They'd get over it with a little time.

"Ladies and gentlemen, a quick word!"

Stone was standing in the middle of the salon. Luckily, J.J. didn't have to answer Libby's coffee question. Stone was going to make a speech or something.

"What's he up to?"

Libby shrugged in answer.

The assembled, well-coiffed, and juicily moisturized guests were all handed flutes of champagne, courtesy of a wait staff that materialized out of nowhere. There was also cheese and little sandwiches. J.J. hadn't ordered any of it. Stone sure knew how to do it up.

They all moved closer to Stone, who looked more and more like a man who fit in Irish Hills—well, if Irish Hills were populated by incredibly well-groomed men.

"I just want to thank you all for helping us soft launch. I have been on the outskirts of this town for around two years, and I have to say, getting to be on the inside of this project and the grocery store has been the most fun I've ever had."

"Come on, you've been to Coachella. We heard that had to be something," J.J. quipped. She couldn't resist a quip.

"It's not. The bathroom situation is awful, trust me," Goldie piped up.

"Coachella notwithstanding, this has been way better. There is one reason for that, and it's J.J."

There was hoot and applause.

J.J. shook her head. "Please, it's a salon, not a military operation."

"Do not let her fool you. She is a general if I've ever seen one." That got some laughs of recognition.

Yet J.J. didn't think of herself as a general of anything. In charge of her kids, the PTA, and, of course, Dean when needed, yes. But the boss? She'd never been that. And here was the boss of all bosses saying she'd taken charge. J.J. felt her face get red with the attention, but also, she felt proud. She *had* whipped this place into shape.

"To J.J.!" Stone said and raised his glass. Her friends and family followed suit.

"Oooh, drink up. He bought the good stuff," Emma called out.

J.J. mingled, and she checked all the final outcomes of her soft clients. Everyone there booked their first official appointments for the coming weeks.

The salon was on its way.

Slowly, people made their way out one by one, and J.J. found herself sweeping up.

"You're not supposed to be the one doing that, boss lady."

"Ah, if you don't want to sweep up, don't get in the salon business. Grab the dustpan."

Stone did as she said, and again, they were happily in the now familiar dance of working together. She was oddly comfortable sweeping dust into Stone Stirling's waiting pan.

"Well, you did it. You pulled it off."

"Amazing what a lot of cash and a deadline can do."

They both walked to the backroom. J.J. leaned the broom by the storeroom door. Stone emptied the dustpan like a pro. She wondered if, a year ago, he'd ever even touched one.

"Oh, hey, you got some hair dye or something there." Stone pointed to his cheek. She rubbed her own, figuring she must look ridiculous.

"Did I get it?"

"No, wait, here." He reached out and smoothed his thumb across her cheek toward her ear.

Like a lightning bolt, she was wrapped in Stone Stirling's arms, and he was kissing her. She kissed him back, and it wasn't a timid first-date kiss. It was a real, grown woman kiss. For a moment, her head was swimming. She forgot where she was, even who she was.

This is one good kiss.

And just as fast as it happened, J.J. stepped back. She had shocked herself.

"I'm sorry, I didn't mean to be inappropriate. I don't know what came over me." Stone lifted both his hands in the air like it was a stickup.

"No, no, I get it all the time. I'm magnetic."

J.J.'s go-to mode was humor. It was her crutch, her shield, her weapon, needed. And in this very uncharted territory, she decided to joke her way out of whatever just happened.

"You are," Stone replied seriously. "You're beautiful and amazing. I just overstepped. My fault entirely."

"Please, this is what happens when you spend too much time with bleach and permanent solution; you're delirious. I'm late, though. I need to get going. Can you—?"

"—Lock up? Sure, of course. Absolutely."

And somehow, J.J. got out of there.
She got in her car and sped away.

* * *

How in the world? What in the world?

Stone had taken the blame. He'd apologized immediately. She knew he didn't have a thing to apologize for. She knew this because she wanted him to kiss her. She had liked it, and now felt a wave of guilt.

She was the one who felt sorry.

How could I? Dean hasn't even been gone a year, and I'm kissing another man! What is wrong with me?

Her grief was overwhelming, and then she turned around and acted like a fool on top of it.

The guilt was all hers, and if she could apologize to Dean, she would.

But Dean was gone. The guilt she felt started to morph into anger.

"Stupid Dean, this is your fault. This is *all* your fault. I am supposed to be calm and settled. We're supposed to be enjoying grandchildren or vacations or whatever. I'm not supposed to be fumbling through a kiss with someone else."

She hit the steering wheel with her palms.

J.J. was too embarrassed to call her friends,ke she did in most situations. They counseled each other, encouraged each other, and were there for each other in moments like this. But the hard truth was that none of them had been through this moment. She was the only widow in the bunch. None of them understood what it felt like to cheat on a husband.

Was it cheating? Had she just cheated?

No. No No, technically not. But the fact that the kiss felt good, that she enjoyed it, that she knew she liked Stone Stirling made her feel worse. Not better.

The day that was supposed to be a triumph was ending in confusion. All she could think was that she wasn't ready to return. To be in the deep end of anything important. Bottom line Libby and D.J. had put J.J. in a position of needing to deal with more than she could handle without Dean.

She didn't want to deal with this town, these people, these memories, and this new reality. She should be in a town where no one knew her, and she had no connections.

She'd not necessarily been happy out on the road, but at least she wasn't in situations like this. She could ride the surface of her emotions and the connections in her life. They were distant. Right now, she was knee-deep in all of it.

And she didn't want to be.

J.J. passed the turnoff to Treach's Cottage. She just needed to drive. So, she did, in circles, around Manitou Lake.

She didn't want to be alone, but she knew that if any of her friends saw her right now, they would know she was discombobulated and totally confused.

"Stupid Dean, this is the way teenagers deal with life. Not middle-aged women. I'm all hot, bothered, guilty, and thinking I will get in trouble. I hope you're happy."

She replayed the moment that Stone and she kissed. And then she squeezed her eyes shut and shook her head.

Chapter Twenty-Two

2002

She'd selected a white carpet for their bedroom. Dean had insisted that she pick what she wanted. But she kept fretting about it. She loved the look of the carpet, but white? Only a movie star or a fool would pick white.

The kids were way too little for there to be a white carpet.

They'd spend years redoing almost every square inch of the house they bought from Jackie. J.J. chose décor on the basis of how it could withstand two little boys, Dean, and Dean's crew.

"Can you just put a cement floor with a drain in the center of it so we can just hose it down every day?" She wasn't really kidding. A garden hose and a drain would be the smart move in just about any room in this place.

"No, but I mean, get brown or Kool-Aid red floors just to be safe."

She had done that, sort of. If she put it in their house, it was tough and could withstand a lot.

But their bedroom carpet was different.

She'd had Dean paint the walls a creamy white. Everything in there looked like the inside of a cloud. But when it came to the carpet, she hesitated.

"You want the white plush? Get the white plush."

Dean wanted her to love the redone bedroom. He wanted her to feel it was hers now, not Jackie's. Every part of the house was all of their house, but this space, he wanted to give her this space.

J.J. relented and selected a plush white carpet for the primary bedroom. It was like walking on a fluffy robe. Dean had installed it that morning, and she'd spent a criminal amount of time making her bed. She'd found all the linens at T.J. Maxx in Jackson. The entire set, plus accent pillows, was under one hundred bucks.

It was rare their bed was made. J.J. and Dean staggered their work shifts as much as they could manage. If she was in bed, Dean was up early on a job. He would get the kids down to sleep many nights as she took evening clients. They saved on childcare that way. Though it meant someone was always going in or going out of that bed.

But this day, this first day with the new primary bedroom, she had everything just so.

The kids were asleep. She was tucked in her new comforter atop her gorgeous plush white carpet.

She fell asleep in her little cloud. She was content, happy, and satisfied now that this was her house, not the remnants of Jackie's chaos.

"Mom. Mom."

J.J.'s eyes flew open. There was little Austin. Standing at her bedside, barefoot on her arctic white plush carpet.

"What?" She'd gone from some dream state to fully alert by the second uttering of Mom.

"BLUURGG."

Pinkish-red former Kool-Aid combined with chicken nugget remnants shot out of Austin's mouth at a high velocity.

"Wait, oh!"

But it was too late. He'd christened the brand-new white carpet.

She scooped him up and carried him to the bathroom. Throwing up scared little ones, and Austin was no different. He cried and threw up again at the same time.

She reassured him he was okay. He didn't feel warm. This wasn't the flu. It was a tummy issue, she decided.

J.J. cleaned him up, got him to sip some water successfully, and then sat on the floor next to him in his room for a bit. The giant bowl used for puke or popcorn was now perched next to his bed. He fell asleep. She touched his forehead to reassure herself this time.

Again. No fever.

Poor thing. The midnight drama had tuckered him out an, and was sleeping soundly now. An hour after the initial wake-up call, she padded back to her room.

"What happened?" Dean asked. He'd slept through the entire situation.

"Austin lost his dinner all over the new carpet."

She looked down. She hadn't thought twice about the carpet in the flurry of settling Austin down.

Dean sat up and looked at the spot. "Ew, is he okay?"

"Yeah."

"I'm afraid that carpet isn't."

"Yeah, so much for the white."

She'd used all kinds of cleaning products, but there was a permanent spot, several actually, where Austin had been.

Eventually, she just bought a throw rug, covered the stain, and called it a failed experiment.

Present Day

. . .

When she answered her phone, the word "Mom" woke her up.

She was immediately awake.

Now, with grown kids, she wished for the days when the worst thing that could wake her in the middle of the night was a red dye stain on the new carpet. When the phone rings at three a.m., there is nothing good on the other end. Nothing.

"Mom."

J.J. was disoriented. She wasn't in her house.

Where is Dean? Where am I? Did I dream that? That I heard my phone?

No, it was in her hand. It was up to her ear.

"Mom."

There it was again.

She was awake now. Totally and frighteningly so. "I'm here. D.J.?"

"I'm okay. But I need your help. I don't know what."

D.J.'s voice was odd. His words were slurred.

The reality clicked in her brain. He was calling her in the dead of night, and he sounded disoriented. He was slurring his words.

She sat up in bed. "What is it?"

"I'm in the ditch. The truck's in the ditch. I don't know what to do. I need you to pick me up."

Has he hit his head? Is this a concussion? Is he bleeding or lightheaded?

"Where? Are you hurt? Was anyone else?"

"No. No. Of course not."

D.J. said he was along some road with the truck in a ditch.

J.J.'s mind leaped to everything awful, everything she feared. "Where. What street?"

She'd get there. She'd be sure he was safe. That was first. Get to her son. "Do you know where you are?"

"Somewhere, out by the dance hall, you know, I'm not sure." D.J. rambled on. She needed him to keep talking. Somehow, having him talk seemed like the right thing.

"Hey! Figure it out. Where are you?"

"I can ping you."

"Just look, is it by a field or closer to the lake?"

"Field, you know how Rexard and Southford come together?"

There were no such roads. But she thought she had an idea what he meant.

She fired questions at him, and at the same time, J.J. found her jeans and a sweatshirt.

My keys, I need my keys. They were in her bag.

In less than five minutes since she'd been awakened from a dead sleep, J.J. was in her car, trying to decide how to proceed. The clock on her dashboard showed it was 3:30 in the morning.

What was the law here? Am I supposed to call the police?

"D.J., you said it was near Rexford and Southard?"

"Yeah, sure. Yeah."

The phone went dead then. He'd hung up or tried to ping her or whatever.

"D.J.!"

She was never one to track her kids with apps or tags. She always felt that was some sort of false sense of security. Like they couldn't get into trouble if you tracked the trouble? But right now, she sure wished she'd have micro-chipped D.J. like they do pets. *Where exactly was he? Was he close to his truck?*

There wasn't another car on the road. She was glad for that. Less likelihood for someone to hit D.J. because they didn't see him. *And God, please make it so he didn't hit anything or anyone else!*

She thanked God he wasn't on 223, where cars drove fast, and no one would expect a pedestrian on the shoulder. Or maybe he *was* on 223?

J.J. needed to find him.

She slowed down when Rexford and Southard met. It was at an angle instead of a standard intersection. *Is that what caused the accident?*

Her eyes scanned the intersection, and there it was.

Her headlights illuminated the taillights of the truck.

Dean's truck. The back end stuck out of the ditch. J.J. slowed down and pulled to the side of the road. The ditch was half-filled with runoff water.

The ditches served an important purpose. They kept the roads from flooding most of the time. But they could be dangerous. Her mind flashed to about a decade ago when a group of kids, playing after a storm, decided to wade in. One was swept under and drowned.

J.J. shook her head to erase the memory of what could happen here.

The front of the truck was smashed into the embankment. The body looked bent. It was a mess.

Where was D.J.? How could he have walked away and called me after this massive car crash?

She looked around. There was no sign of him.

"D.J.!" she called out.

No answer. J.J. got back in her car. She drove along the road slowly, with her eyes scanning toward the tree line on Southard.

D.J. was on foot. He'd said that.

She called his phone again. It went to voice mail.

"You've reached Tucker Construction. Leave a message, and we'll get back to you ASAP. Thank you!"

It was Dean's voice. D.J. had taken Dean's business phone and never changed the greeting. It felt like a gut punch.

"I need some help here, Dean, really."

Something caught her eye up ahead. It wasn't moving. *Oh God, what if he's hurt? What if he got hit or hit his head?*

She pulled closer and saw it was a man, her son. She just knew it.

J.J. pulled over. She was careful to put her car in park. She needed to keep her head. There was no Dean to help.

No matter what she found, she'd have to deal with it.

The roadside gravel shifted under her shoes as she ran to D.J.

He was on his side.

"D.J."

He moved when he heard her voice.

Okay, he moved. He is alive.

Just that fact flooded her with relief.

She kneeled down next to him, looking for anything broken or bleeding. Her headlights were the only light in the dead of night.

But they were enough. He was in one piece. There didn't seem to be blood.

"D.J."

He rolled from his side and opened his eyes. She needed to figure out what to do next. *How do I fix this? We need to get to the emergency room? The police?*

"Mom, hey, what are you doing here?"

"You called me, remember? You crashed your truck."

"What, no, me and the boys were out." He had a smile on his face.

She was cold inside when he smiled. It was clear now. Crystal clear in the dark of night.

D.J. had gotten behind the wheel drunk as a skunk. He'd driven his truck into the ditch. Drunk. Her mind played every possible horrible consequence.

Her fear for his safety shifted into fear of a million other scenarios.

"Did you crash into anything else? Do you know?"

"Crash? No, no, just tired, ma."

"Get up." She said it in her field-general mad-as-hell voice.

Because her terror had turned to anger. She was mad now. Mad and in a low-grade panic. She stood up, put her hand out, and helped him to his feet. He staggered, and she tried to steady him.

"Get in my car, now, here, come on."

She tucked herself under his arm and got him to the car. He opted for the back seat and laid down. His legs were hanging out of the door when she tried to close it.

"Bend. BEND."

He did as she said, and she was able to get his door closed.

She knew what the first call had to be.

"Patrick. Yeah, it's J.J. I got a mess, and I don't know exactly what to do first."

"Always call a lawyer first, you know that."

"Yeah, I do."

She explained the situation and that Greg McQueen was on the way.

"Okay, I'm on the way too. I'll be there in less than five minutes. Anyone else shows up before me, you two keep your mouths shut."

"Sure." She had no idea what D.J.'s capacity for conversation or instruction would be by the time this hit the fan.

* * *

She was still standing next to the car several minutes later when headlights hit her face.

"D.J., get up. Can you?"

"Yep, yep. Sure can."

Patrick Tate stepped out of his car. She was low key relieved that he hadn't brought Emma with him. The two were joined at the hip.

"Saw the truck, busted up good. I'll take care of that. And this one. You get on home."

"Are you sure?"

"Yep. D.J., get in my car."

D.J. looked at her.

"Deej, just do what Patrick says." She put a hand on his shoulder and patted it.

"I'll touch base tomorrow."

"Good. I'm going to have some other legal-type questions by then, I expect."

Chapter Twenty-Three

J.J. drove back home to Treach's cottage.

She still had D.J.'s phone, and that was on purpose.

She felt a little strange, opening it. But it was too late to turn back now. She was cleaning up this mess. This didn't mean picking up crumbs with tweezers; it meant getting out the push broom and taking a bath.

She opened the phone, and she could see tons of personal calls. Of course, D.J.'s books were a mess; no surprise that he'd muddied the use of a personal phone and a business phone.

She sorted through messages, missed calls, and emails from Libby. There were a *lot* of emails from Libby. The trail of correspondence from Libby painted a picture of a woman getting increasingly frustrated and desperate. Libby was trying to keep D.J. in business, but D.J. kept dropping the ball. Over and over again. J.J. felt overwhelming shame that she'd doubted Libby. Libby had been right. Libby was mothering D.J., too.

The work he'd done was good, but getting him to do the work, getting him to respond, getting him sober, that was the challenge. A major town project had hinged on Dean Tucker Construction and was falling apart without him.

J.J. had been angry at Libby, thinking her friend had been too hard on her son. But she was wrong. Libby had been doing all she could to keep D.J. on the job. To keep the Tucker family business alive. She had amends to make with Libby.

She would. But first, she had to save Tucker Construction. D.J. had tangled it into knots. She was going to have to spend all her time smoothing it back out.

J.J. didn't go back to bed. She showered, though, and brewed coffee. There was a lot of work to do. She needed to get to the trailer and talk to the electrical contractor, and there was an order of tile—*that darn tile!* There were loose ends everywhere.

She poured the coffee into a traveling mug.

She'd have to have several important conversations soon. Maybe even today. But the sunrise over the lake called her out.

Every day on the lake, the sunrise was a different color. This morning, it was purple on the horizon with a few dappled clouds. They were dark but not threatening.

A swish alerted her to her neighbor, Mama Swan.

"Oh, good morning, mama."

She'd never seen the male swan again. It likely died from the injury it suffered while trying to free the female from the dock. But now, the mama had five little cygnets to manage.

"Would you look at that!"

The mama swam slowly near the shore. Her feathers were brilliant white, but her cygnets were still dusty gray. They'd turn white later in the year.

Her five babies nestled on her back. All at the same time. J.J. had seen the mama before, with one on her back and the others swimming around. But this was special. The mama had room for all of them. Though there was some cygnet jockeying and adjusting, it was mostly a peaceful means of transport for the babies. Her two big wings provided a cradle for them. They snuggled and peeked out over her feathers at the water. The mama glided smoothly with her family tucked in safely behind her.

"I'll be back later today with some treats, how's that sound?"
The mama swan glided further away.

* * *

She was in the construction trailer thirty minutes later when Patrick rang.

"So, do I want to know?"

"He's square with the law. The truck is in Arrow's garage. Looked pretty totaled to me."

"I'll check on it. Square with the law?"

"It's handled and all above board. He's going to head to rehab, but that's a conversation you'll want to have."

J.J. wanted to feel relief about rehab, but she also knew the road D.J. was on was long and harder than he understood.

At least he hadn't hurt anyone. That was the thing that she held on to.

Shortly after midday, D.J. appeared in the trailer. He filled the small space with his broad shoulders. But they were hunched over.

Has he learned a lesson?

"Mom, I'm so sorry."

"Yeah, I'm sure." She'd decided how she'd handled D.J. had been wrong. Twice wrong.

A part of her wanted to tell him all was well. She wanted to make it go away, this problem. But it wasn't hers to solve. Just like Dean's wasn't hers to solve.

"I'm taking over," she told him.

"Sure, Patrick said it's a six-week program, so I can swing back in afterward. If you can manage."

"D.J., this isn't your business to run. I'm running it. For the foreseeable future."

"What?"

"I made a mistake leaving. I can see that. You had a lot on your plate. For that, I'm sorry. But when I came, I didn't want to see the truth. I do now."

"Don't you think you're being dramatic? This was one time. One mistake."

"It was a lucky break, the way I see it. You're still walking, and you didn't kill anyone. But luck isn't a plan for life. Or this business."

He winced at her words. They were true. But she knew it was hard to hear. And laying down the law with her son was ten times harder than it had been with Dean all those years ago.

"I'm sorry. I'll make it right. This place. Everything."

She broke a little then, seeing how young he looked. She took his hands in hers.

"The only thing you need to do is to be honest with yourself. You're sick. But you have the ability to get better. Go get better."

"Okay, Mom. I'm going to try."

They stood up. She hugged him. She didn't cry, though. Not in front of him. D.J. had seen enough of her soft side in the last few weeks. Softness wasn't going to help.

"Patrick's taking me, so I'll talk to you when I can."

She nodded. "I love you."

"Love you, too," he said as he walked out of the trailer and to Patrick's car. She watched her oldest boy walk across the street. She turned away.

There were still miles to go to get things sorted away.

Chapter Twenty-Four

"I need your help. Yep. No, you can finish what you need to, but no more slow rolling this out. This is how it's going to play out over the next few weeks."

J.J.'s conversation with Austin was very different from the one she'd had with D.J. Austin was going to start tomorrow and be here on the job. He was no more ready to take over the construction business than D.J. was, but he was of sound body right now. And he needed to learn the ropes of Tucker Construction.

By the time the sun went down, J.J. had a handle on the next few days of obligations and a better picture of what needed to be done for Libby. She'd meet with Libby later, but she knew she'd have to eat crow, as they say. So, she'd avoid it for a few more hours at least.

Plus, J.J. had no less than four missed calls from Stone. She saw the light at the salon was on, and it was time to have another tough conversation.

Lila was at the reception desk.

"Aunt J.J.! We've been swamped today. Totally nuts. We're booked for the next month."

"Wow, that's excellent. And the app is working with the scheduling for each of the stylists?"

"Yep, perfectly. I had to do an update this morning, but that was fine."

"Good."

The Do was rolling; there were three ladies in the chairs, and it looked like a pedi was underway as J.J. passed by and headed for the backroom.

There, she found Stone Stirling, an internationally famous billionaire, twisting a garbage bag and tying it off.

He looked like he belonged there. And like he'd done it before.

"Hey! There you are! I called. I was worried that I had totally scared you off."

He lowered his voice when he said it. The best place for great gossip was a salon. She'd warned him multiple times about that. She just didn't think she'd be at the center of any juicy gossip.

"Scare me? Nah, no. But we do need to talk."

"Yeah, want to take a walk? Since the stylists all do have ears."

"Yes, perfect."

They walked out back and down the sidewalk a bit. The gazebo in the center of town was a good place to sit. She knew it was a tribute to Dean, so maybe it was good he was there with them. Sort of.

"I want to apologize, but I can't," Stone said once they were settled.

"What?"

"I kissed you. And I was contrite, but I got to thinking about it last night, and what do the kids say? Sorry, not sorry."

"Ah, so cocky. That's on brand."

"No, it's just I wanted to kiss you for months. And I can't feel bad about that."

"Well, then." She wasn't used to this sort of full-court press courting. *Is it courting?*

"And it was a great kiss. Best one I've ever been a part of."

"Now you're making me blush." She was grateful for the fading evening light. J.J. Tucker was not supposed to be shy!

"Look, I'm not sorry. But I am also not a cad. If you want to take over the salon, and I've now made it uncomfortable, I will step aside. Immediately. I realized that could be why you've said no to officially taking the reins. I'm too much, or you're weirded out."

"Thank you. That's generous." Somewhere between The Do's opening night and navigating the mess at Tucker Construction, J.J. Tucker knew what she wanted. She knew exactly what she wanted.

"Whatever you want to do, you're the boss."

"Ha, so, I am—or want to be—but not at the salon. I've been in salons for nearly thirty years. What I want now is to make sure Tucker Construction survives. Thrives, actually."

"Well, well, well, all this time, I thought you were a budding Estee Lauder, but you're really a construction magnate!"

"Don't get me wrong, if you mess up that salon, I'll be back so fast it will blow your toupee off."

"I thought we went over this."

"Kidding. I'll help you interview managers if you'd like. But I'm trading the blow dryer for a backhoe or something like that."

"That actually is no surprise. There doesn't seem to be anything you can't do."

She put out her hand, and he took it in his. "So, one thing I'm not good at yet is this. I felt like I was cheating on my husband. I mean, I liked the kiss, but I thought I was going to be smote from above all the way home."

"You're dumping me?"

"No, I'm putting the brakes on for a little bit. I want us to stay friends."

"Ouch."

"No...you know."

"I do know," Stone said earnestly. "And J.J. Tucker. I'm not going anywhere."

"Good, it will be easier to spy on you that way."

"What?"

"You know that was my job, spy on your activities for Libby?"

"She's always working, that one."

"But you turned me into a double agent."

"HA!"

They sat for a while, in the gazebo, hand in hand.

Thanks to them, the town would have a month's worth of juicy gossip.

* * *

Back at Treach's cottage that night, J.J. put on Dean's old buffalo plaid flannel. And she talked to him like he was there with her.

She confessed she might start dating. And she explained the situation with their sons.

"Dean, I dropped the ball on D.J., but hopefully, he takes this second chance. Like you did. Like we did."

She'd tried to run away from her memories of him. Because it hurt. Running hadn't been the answer. It hurt then, too.

With time, she hoped it would hurt less. In time, maybe she'd be able to smile when she thought of their life together. She tested it out.

"Remember that time Austin barfed all over the new white carpet?"

J.J. vowed to get braver with her memories. She'd open old albums and think of beautiful moments, too, in time.

Right now, even the silly memories brought a flood of tears welling up in her eyes.

She pulled the flannel around her, and she let the tears come.

Chapter Twenty-Five

June
Stone

She wanted to fly commercial.

"Dad, a private jet is wasteful. And I don't need it." Somehow, Averil Stone had become the opposite of a brat. He could only say it was her mother and her stepdad because Stone had barely been an influence.

He tried to send his private plane to pick her up and bring her here. But she refused. She said she wanted to ask something, to request something in person. Stone's answer was yes, how high, and is it too late?

Avvie also refused his offer to pick her up at the airport. Their relationship was tentative. Polite. But no question it was distant. He was doing what he could to change that. But that also meant not insisting on taking care of everything.

J.J. was teaching him how to let things happen between people. Patience.

"Stone, the way we continue to progress is just time spent.

You're going to have to spend time with your daughter. And the rest will come." J.J. was talking about Avvie but also the two of them. He'd learned he found joy in just being in Irish Hills. He found a better version of himself, being a part of their plans instead of the boss. He could help when he saw the need but also had space to watch people decide what they wanted. And they made it happen.

J.J. continued to let him spend time with her as they interviewed managers for the salon and as he consulted with her on the renovations Tucker Construction would oversee for the Dance Hall that Goldie and Stone Stirling Foundation were funding. Goldie wanted to turn it into a venue again for concerts, weddings, and her film festival idea. He was writing the checks and gleefully working with J.J. as she managed the construction aspect with her sons. The day-in and day-out ebb and flow in one community deepened his relationships with the people in his life.

He also needed to find a way to be a part of his daughter's life. But she was about to start her medical residency. She was an adult. She was obviously independent. Well, at least maybe she'd see the charm of Irish Hills and visit once a year. His place on Lake Manitou was huge and had plenty of space for her. Heck, it had an embarrassing amount of space. Funny how he never used to think about filling rooms before. When J.J. showed up with the Sandbar Sisters and their picture of whatever J.J. had concocted, he was the happiest he'd ever been.

He'd used her recipe for green juice, aka, a margarita lime, and had it all set up for Avvie's arrival.

He sat on the back deck and watched the water. A pontoon floated by, and then a speed boat with a skier. Keith Brady told him he'd need to learn to ski if he was going to keep up in the summer with this crew. He was looking forward to the lesson.

"Dad?"

He heard her call and turned to see Avvie, tall and beautiful, standing on the steps to the back deck.

"Honey, you made it!" He walked over and hugged her. She seemed surprised. She hugged him back, but it was reserved. They were strangers, really.

"This is so pretty. I can see why you have made this your home base."

"Yes, I think it's a hidden little pocket of the country. I almost ruined it. But the people here set me straight. After a bit. Destroyed me a few times, actually."

"I have a hard time believing that."

"Let me take your bag."

"Don't you have, uh, someone for that?"

"No, I admit, I have a housekeeper and, of course, a couple of assistants for the business, but no butler these days."

"Wow, other people get red corvettes for their mid-life crisis, and you got, well, you got less douchy. Congrats."

He winced at the word but took it as a compliment.

"Here, let's sit for a second. I've made a couple of drinks for us."

Avvie walked over to the deck chairs and looked out at the lake. She sat down, and Stone handed her a drink. He sat down beside her.

"I don't know what kind of time you have, but we can go to town for dinner. Or I can take the little boat out there to my friend's place. He's got a lovely dockside restaurant."

"Both sound great, whatever. But, before you do, I need to ask you a favor."

"Anything, you know that." He was instantly worried. She never asked for anything. She never wanted for anything, financially at least. The rest of her needs were met by her mother. She'd never needed a thing from him.

"Well, you know it was match day a couple months back."

"Yes, your mother told me you were successful and that you'd call and let me know. I missed that call."

"Yeah, that's on me. I was floundering a bit. She wanted me to call you right away. Said you owed me. But that's not how I wanted to play it."

Stone shifted in his seat. He didn't want to know about his ex-wife's conversations with Avvie about him. Had they all been negative? Was Avvie's only view of Stone through her mother's lens? Probably.

He held his tongue and let her continue.

"I'm matched at Bixby."

"What? Bixby here, in Lenawee County?"

"Yes."

"How in the world don't you have to put a location in? You live in Seattle. How did you wind up around the corner from here?"

"I asked for it. My grades, tests, and interviews were all good. The algorithms gave me my pick, they say."

"Okay, so you picked a small rural hospital?"

"I don't want to disappoint you, but I don't want to be in Seattle, New York, or L.A. anymore. I love Mom, but not the places she likes to be. And when you told me about this place. Well, I decided it sounded good for a couple of reasons."

"It is good. Great, really."

Stone could scarcely believe what he was hearing. It was the best news he'd ever gotten.

"But I don't have a place to stay."

Stone wanted to leap to his feet, pick up his baby girl, and squeeze her tight. He wanted to thank her for choosing to be close to him. He had a thousand things to ask her, to show her.

But he thought of J.J.'s advice about letting time and togetherness forge the bond.

"If you'd like to stay here. I'd be honored. There's a lot of space. You'd never even have to see me if you don't want to."

"Hmm. Well, seeing as I decided to move across the country to this little town to get to know my dad, I think I would like to see you. Every once in a while, between hospital shifts. If you're okay with it."

"I think it's the best thing I've ever heard."

They sat for a few more minutes and drank J.J.'s green juice.

"Whoa, this is strong."

"Yeah, another friend says it's the only way to make a margarita."

"Am I going to get to meet some of these friends?"

"Actually, if you want to, we can get in the boat now and join a few for burgers."

"Burgers? Stone Stirling is eating burgers dockside in the Midwest on a Friday night?"

"Yep. We've got a lot to catch up on."

"Seems like we do."

"I've discovered that dockside in the Midwest is a really good place to do just that."

Chapter Twenty-Six

July 3rd
J.J.

"It's a Chamber of Commerce Day, Libby," Viv said as all five of them—Goldie, Viv, Hope, Libby, and J.J.—found their spot near the sandbar. Goldie had learned how to captain her fancy pontoon boat without her handsome handyman. He was there for when she wanted to bring it back to the dock.

Aunt Emma was on the porch of Nora House. She said she wanted to watch from the shade. J.J. knew Aunt Emma would get her toes in if it got too hot.

"For my money, July 4th is for amateurs. Today is the day," J.J. said.

The lake would be crowded tomorrow. Nora House would be packed with their friends and family, but today, July 3rd, it was just them. Even Hope, who hated leaving the restaurant, was here. She'd packed the cooler with goodies. They planned to be on the lake all day.

"Push the button. That's all you have to do. Push the button!"

Goldie said, and Viv did as instructed. The awning covered the boat.

Back in the day, they'd be straining to get every drop of sun. Today, they slathered every drop of sunscreen.

"Are we close enough?" Hope asked as she looked into the water.

"We're going to swim to it a little bit. We need the exercise," Goldie said.

J.J. looked at her friends. She saw them as they were, back in the day: young, gorgeous, full of dreams. Some of those dreams had come true. Others had not. They'd also all found new dreams and new loves, but always the old friends.

"So, it's getting serious with Cole and Siena," Goldie said.

"How serious?" Hope asked.

"Serious enough that I have looked at mother-of-the-bride dresses for Goldie and for me and am not impressed. I'm going to take a crack at designing some and put them on a rack at Just the Thing." Viv said, and she would probably revolutionize mother of the bride dresses if her track record was any indication.

"Whatever you do will be better than all that light blue chiffon. We're Gen X, and the dresses out there are for our grandmothers. We're not grandmothers," Goldie said.

"Yet, any day now, ladies, any day," Hope said.

"How's Julia doing?" Viv asked.

"Great, she's going to spend her last few weeks with me, just in case." Hope's daughter Julia was about to make Hope a grandma for the first time.

"Can you believe it? Grandmas? We're grandmas," Libby said.

"I can believe it. I hurt my neck sleeping last week. Sleeping! How do you do that?" J.J. said. She didn't want Austin or D.J. to make her a grandma just yet. They were still in need of sorting.

"Is D.J. coming tomorrow?" Libby asked.

"I think so, in the early part of the day. But beer, you know, there'll be a lot of it. So, he's going to see us in the morning and go to a meeting. He said."

D.J. had been home for one week. All seemed well so far. She'd made Austin his supervisor, so she was sure they'd eventually start fighting. But she knew Austin would handle it.

"Well, I'm glad he's back on the job. I missed him," Libby said and reached out to squeeze J.J.'s hand.

Libby was like a mom to J.J.'s cubs, and J.J. still kicked herself for doubting it.

"Okay, enough complaining about our old bones. I'm getting in!" Viv whipped off her kaftan and stood on the edge of the pontoon. She performed a perfectly awkward cannonball. "Oh wow, it's perfect in here!"

Goldie and Hope followed. Libby was next.

J.J. was the last on the boat. The girls were kicking and splashing and had made their way to the sandbar.

They'd spent their childhood together, these girls, and they had drifted so far apart as women, but one by one, they'd all come back.

J.J. looked back up to the porch of Nora House. Aunt Emma waved at her. Aunt Emma had lured Libby home.

"The town needs you girls, mark my words, J.J. I'm going to get them all back here."

At the time, J.J. thought Emma was losing her marbles. How wrong she was. Aunt Emma had masterminded it, really. What a gift Emma had given them in each other.

Libby, Hope, Goldie, and Viv were almost to the sandbar.

"Come on, J.J.!" Libby called. "I told you the water's good."

Goldie was already arranging herself, Viv was soaking in the sun, and Hope did a somersault in the water.

J.J. jumped into the lake and joined her sisters on the sandbar.

Chapter Twenty-Seven

Emma Ford Libby

The girls were out there, sunning themselves on the raft. Just like the old days.

Emma had her turn on the raft. The radio played *I've Got a Gal in Kalamazoo* and *Tangerine* when it was her turn.

The Sandbar Sisters had theirs, with that silly group, what was it? Wham. That made her giggle, Wham!

Very soon, there'd be a new generation of feet splashing in the water and baby toes squishing in the sand.

She smiled. She could see it even though it hadn't come to pass yet. Days at the lake were the same today as the days when her father first brought them here.

No matter what Mother Nature or Father Time threw at them, Irish Hills had survived. Lake Manitou was still here for those new generations. She'd seen to it!

This was what she'd orchestrated. Emma did not have any illusion that at her age she could have saved the town on her own. But she knew who to call and how to get things done when it mattered.

Emma also knew how to make the best lemonade. It was her mother's recipe. Her beautiful mother Nora Sullivan. She had a pitcher on the porch table. It was ready for the girls when they swam back.

Ma, Nora Sullivan, maid turned matriarch. How she missed her Ma. But the taste of the lemonade, the fragrance of the hydrangeas growing along the porch, grandchildren of the hydrangeas Nora had tended one hundred years ago, all brought Nora to mind.

Nora would be amazed by Libby and all the Sandbar Sisters. She wouldn't be surprised that they were strong, Nora was strong in that same way. She'd raised Emma to be the same.

Nora Sullivan would be amazed that the women were the town's leaders. They built it, not just nurtured it. They protected it, not just decorated it. The Sandbar Sisters were smart enough to know that a swim in this lovely lake on the Fourth of July was as close to paradise as one got on earth.

Lucky. Grateful. Those were the things Emma felt as she rested on the porch. She leaned her head back in the rocking chair. Maybe she'd doze off a little.

The thought crossed her mind that she would like this to be the last thing she saw before seeing Ma. Emma looked over to the porch stairs. It was Ma, in her white summer dress, hair up. That coppery red hair was so beautiful, the same color as Libby's.

"Ma, it's my time. Yes?"

"No, child. Not yet. You're going to have a visitor and they need your help. Not yet, child." Ma's lovely Irish lilt. No one had that lilt anymore.

Emma sat up. Her Ma was gone.

And there he was. The visitor.

"Aunt Emma, I'd like to ask for her hand in marriage. I want to do it right and get permission."

Emma shook off the blanket of sleep.

Ma was right.
She was about to be very busy!
Weddings didn't plan themselves!

Haven Beach Series

Haven Beach Series
   Find your spot on the hammock and enjoy this women's fiction saga with warm sand, sweet friends, and amazing women who discover ocean breezes can bring second chances. Welcome to Haven Beach where sisters, mothers, daughters, and friends share the humor and heart that make life beautiful. If you like a touch of sweet romance, flip-flops, salt air, and sun on your shoulders, you'll love *Gulfside Girls*.

Also by Rebecca Regnier

Summer Cottage Novels

- Sandbar Sisters
- Sandbar Season
- Sandbar Summer
- Sandbar Storm
- Sandbar Sunrise

Haven Beach Beachy Women's Fiction Series

- Gulfside Girls
- Gulfside Inn
- Gulfside Secret

About the Author

Rebecca Regnier is a television host and award-winning columnist. She lives in Michigan with her family and handsome dog. Follow her on one of her socials. She loves to share laughs with her readers!

- tiktok.com/@rebeccaregnier
- facebook.com/rlregnier
- instagram.com/rebeccaregnier
- amazon.com/stores/Rebecca-Regnier/author/B006NPZDQW

Made in United States
North Haven, CT
20 March 2024